THE IMMORTALS OF SCIENCE FICTION

ISBN 0 8317 4880 X
LOC 80-82168

Designed by Julie Harris & Steve Ridgeway
Assisted by Jill Gambold

Manufactured in Singapore.
First American edition.

THE IMMORTALS OF SCIENCE FICTION

DAVID WINGROVE

MAYFLOWER BOOKS · NEW YORK CITY

INTRODUCTION
ELEVEN

SUSAN CALVIN
THIRTEEN

THE ILLUSTRATED MAN
TWENTY THREE

SLIPPERY JIM DIGRIZ
THIRTY THREE

OSCAR GORDON
FORTY THREE

LEWIS ORNE
FIFTY THREE

ESAU CAIRN
SIXTY THREE

BEOWULF SHAEFFER
SEVENTY THREE

WINSTON SMITH
EIGHTY THREE

WINSTON RUMFOORD
NINETY ONE

HOWARD LESTER
ONE HUNDRED AND ONE

EPILOGUE
ONE HUNDRED AND NINE

ACKNOWLEDGEMENTS
ONE HUNDRED AND THIRTEEN

9

·INTRODUCTION·

On a March morning in 1980, a young Scotsman, Andrew Muir, stepped onto a train at Victoria Station in London, his destination Rome. Sitting in an empty carriage late at night as the train hurtled through the countryside north of Lyons he had the sudden sensation of being surrounded by shadows of his past and future selves. Focusing upon this strange phenomenon he gradually realised that he had stumbled upon the gateway not only to Time, but to the whole continuum of alternate universes that fan out like thin layers of skin to either side of our own. When the train pulled into Lyons station the carriage was empty: Muir was somewhere else.

On a March morning almost thirty thousand years later, I was sitting in Muir's office in the *Daniel Martin* building on G82, an alternate Earth where, as on so many of the probability worlds, Man had not evolved beyond a Neanderthal stage. Muir looked little older than he had been thirty millenia earlier – the scientific discoveries of countless worlds and countless ages had provided him with the means to achieve virtual immortality. On his part he had selected students from the multitude of places he had visited and brought them back to G82 to learn the disciplines whereby they too could travel between the universes and the ages of Earth and its surrounding galaxy.

I was a graduate student of Muir's college and, as I sat there patiently waiting while he scanned the visual display of my qualifications and specialist abilities, wondered what my first assignment would be. He did not keep me waiting very long With a wry smile he looked up over his thin-rimmed glasses (an eccentric affectation he was noted for and recognised by) and began to speak.

"From our privileged perspective, you and I know that not only is the universe infinite *in size,* but also that it is infinite *in number.* Infinity implies the capacity for anything to happen; *anything at all*! Back on Earth-Prime there were a few people who realised this *in theory,* but no one, until I 'stepped away' from that Rome Express, who had *experienced it.*"

He paused, removing his glasses and wiping them on a small cloth he kept in his top pocket for that purpose.

"I recall that we had a thing called 'fiction' back on Earth-Prime; something that supposedly differed from fact in that it was a product of the *imagination* and therefore *not real.* What we didn't know then was that whatever we could imagine – however bizarre that might be – must happen *somewhere* in this or another of the universes *because* of the nature of Infinity. What we didn't realise was that our ability to *imagine* was really only a fragment of our ability to actually *see* other times and other days. Because of our belief in the rigid division between *fact* and *fiction* we stunted our natural ability to travel between the universes and backward and forward in time."

He laughed and handed me the dossier that had lain in front of him on the desk throughout the interview.

"You know most of this, anyway. Your assignment is to track down these ten people and find out a little more than is known from the dossier. Back on Earth-Prime there was a part of their 'fiction' termed '*science fiction*'. All ten of these people were popular 'characters' in sf and were believed to be the products of the *imaginations* of their authors."

"It should be fun," I said, trying to visualise this strange superstition of Earth-Prime. Fiction! What would they believe in next! Later, having read through the dossier, I understood the reasons for my extensive training in *psi*, for the course in "guile and fraud", for the rigorous physical training in all of the ancient martial arts. I was an expert in linguistics and mathematics and my political theory was second-to-none. Confident in my ability to cope with this assignment I relaxed into my chair and assumed the first attitude of the Muir discipline, concentrating upon the ancient superstition-ridden world of Earth-Prime. Fiction! It was my last thought as I slipped out of the matrix of G82.

·SUSAN CALVIN·

With impatience I followed the official guide, hardly bothering to listen to his enthusiastic explanations of the processes whereby a positronic brain was first created and then endowed with a working memory and indoctrinated with the Three Laws of Robotics. In my pocket was the compact edition of "US Robots: Corporation to Empire" by Professor Tony Oudot, the book that traced the important role played by the company in Mankind's expansion throughout the Galaxy. If I had shown it to my guide he might either have been amazed or have thought me mad. It would not be published for a further four hundred years.

I was on the standard tour of the US Robots' laboratories and construction plant just outside of New York, one of a group of six inquisitive sightseers who had paid the requisite five thousand credits for a day spent in the most advanced scientific establishment in the world of 2011.

I found the guide's description of the primitive cybernetic engineering rather tiresome. I had not entered this universe to listen to his mechanical explanations: I had come to meet and talk to US Robots' robopsychologist, the twenty-nine year old Dr Susan Calvin.

We had visited the laboratory she shared with Dr Albert Lanning, US Robots' director of research, earlier in the morning and I had noticed then the coldness of her manner and the precision with which she answered our stumbling queries. It was she who had dealt with us, clipboard in her left hand and her right hand on her hip, while Dr Lanning continued his work on the prototype SPD robot (just out of the design stage, she explained). Her manner suggested that our presence there was a distraction she could well do without – another imposition upon her time by the Public Relations boys in their Manhattan offices. I had kept silent until we had been about to leave, then I asked a carefully prepared question about the effects of selenium upon plantinumiridium and noticed the abrupt change in her attitude, as though she had only just become aware of my presence in the room. She seemed to look through me, as if there were nothing substantial about me except my question. Her cold grey eyes calmly assessed me and then her lips almost formulated a smile. Almost. I never did see Dr Calvin smile. But my

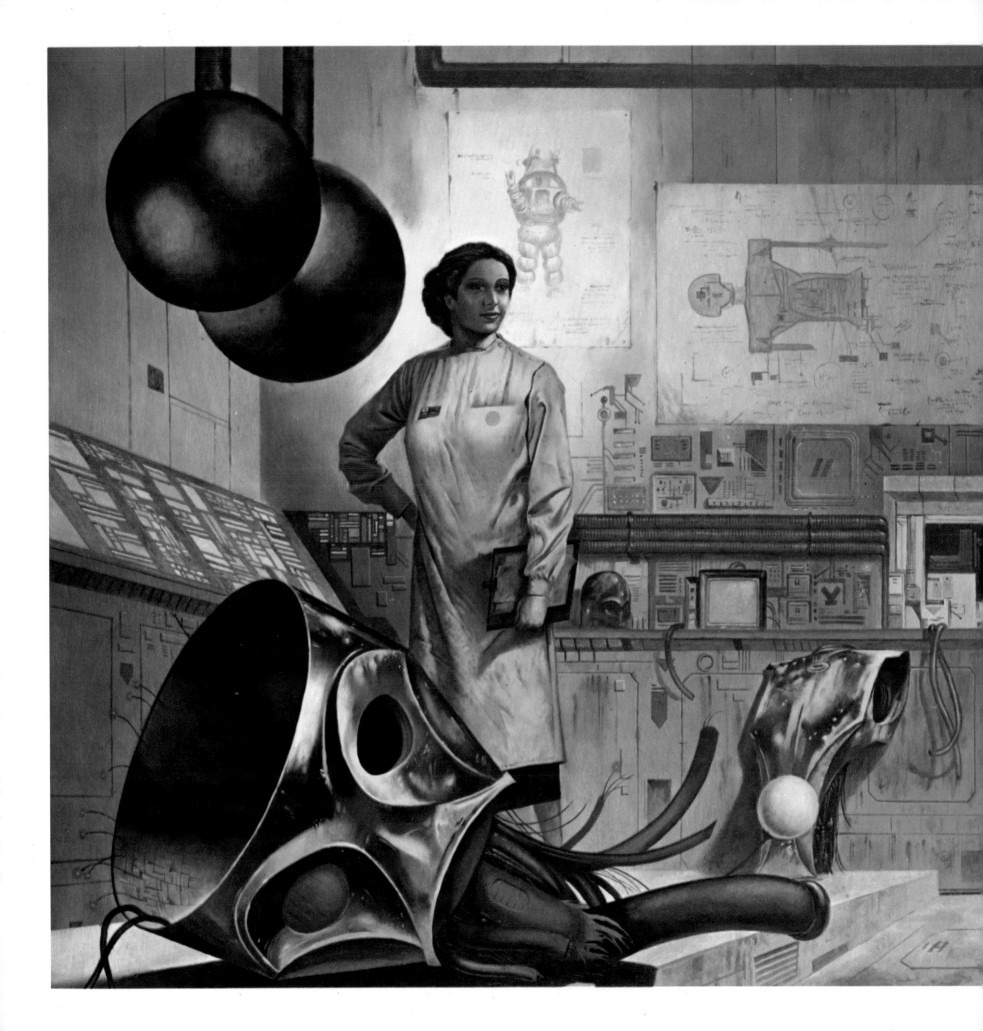

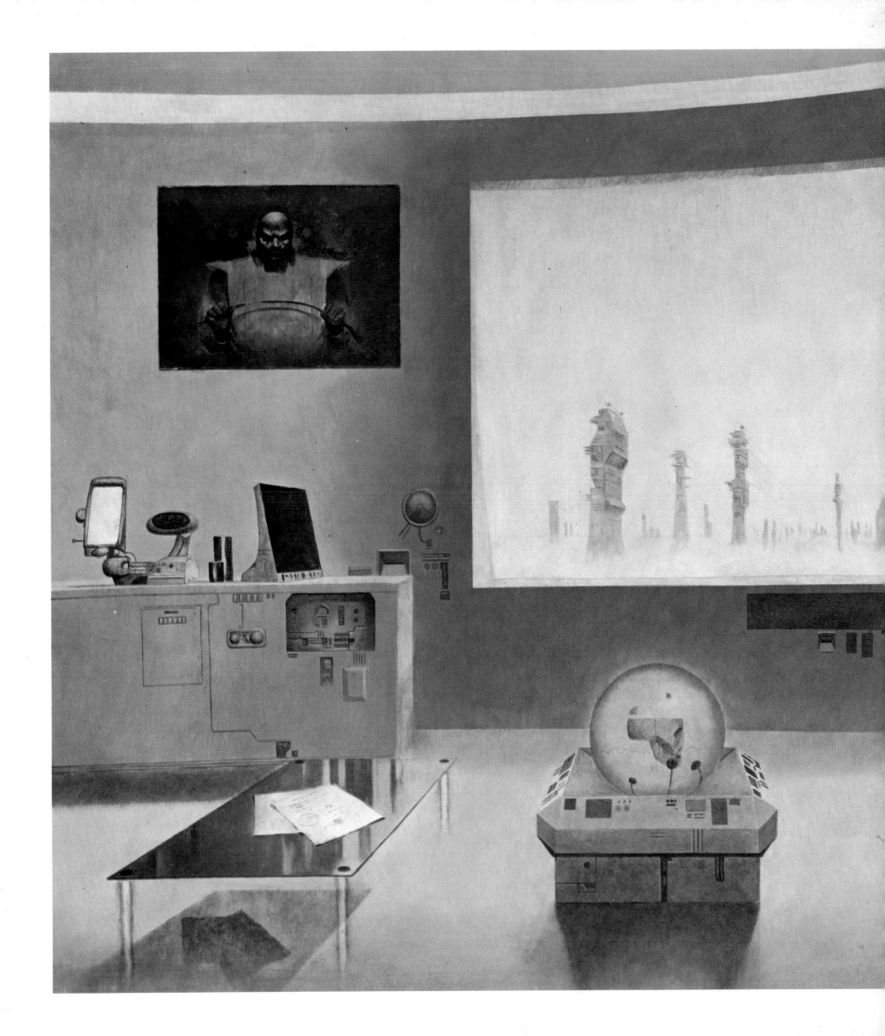

question had its desired effect: at the informal cocktail party in the evening she sought me out and took me into one of the administrative offices on the same floor. There we talked 'science' (being careful to avoid displaying my superior knowledge of humanoid-technology). I managed to discover something of her early life and of the things which had motivated her to dedicate her life to creating a perfect partner for Mankind.

When she was born, in 1982, cybernetics was still very much in its infancy, and she had grown up in a world where Toffler's 'future shock' was as evident as the progression of the seasons. Man needed help, it seemed, if he were not to be swamped by the products of his own technology. As an eight-year-old girl, she had won a National Essay Competiton for her entry, "If Man Is To Cope" (*There is no record of this in any popular account of Dr Calvin's life and it seems she told this item of information to me alone – an indication to me of her fundamental and profound modesty, for it would have been a perfect rejoinder to those unsympathetic critics of hers who often accused her of being as uncaring and inhuman as her metal 'friends'*). In that youthful essay was the whole weight of her idealism – the urgent desire in her to participate in creating a mechanical 'servant' class which could free Man from life's drudgery and allow him to share in the riches of the universe. She had read Mary Shelley's FRANKENSTEIN as a precocious five-year old and dismissed it as arrant Luddite nonsense ("The sort of thing these newly-formed Fundamentalists forever harp on about" *she said, a trace of anger entering her normally dispassionate voice*). Robots to her younger self had been marvellous instruments, and like all instruments had the potential for both good and bad. It was the scientist's task, she had felt, to ensure that the Robot became a humanitarian instrument – a tool for the furtherance of Man's happiness. It was an ideal she was still convinced of. (*As she spoke she clenched her finely-boned hands tightly together, a blush of red forming at her fingertips, contrasting against the normal porcelain whiteness of her skin.*)

"It wasn't that I never *had* any friends. It was simply that I never *needed* any. They were always preoccupied with something outdoors – swimming, cycling, tennis. I was never interested in sports, even though I keep myself – even now – as physically fit as I can, and I've always found – right from the age of three or four – that I was driven by a desire to *know* about things. Pure scientific curiosity . . . something that I guess is almost religious in its intensity, though not of the kind that could be contained in a church. No, what I feel is, I imagine, something like that feeling Einstein experienced – that there's an order – he called it 'God' – behind everything. I guess this work is an extension of that

Plate 1. *In 2011, in the Advanced Robotics laboratory of U.S. Robots & Mechanical Men Inc., Dr Alfred Lamming tests a faulty arm mechanism on the new SPD robot while the young Dr Susan Calvin explains the problems of cybernetic control systems to a guided tour group (out of picture).*

Plate 2. *With the jutting, mile-high towers of Boston showing through the window of her penthouse apartment, Dr Susan Calvin sips wine and tells our investigator of her aim to create an ethical robot. Her robot-domo, Jimmy (JME) attends her. In the foreground a model plantinumiridium brain glows softly.*

feeling: an attempt to make practical some of those early ideals."

That was perhaps the only opportunity I had, or was ever likely to have, of hearing Dr Susan Calvin talk in so direct and unembarrassed a manner about her motivations. There are factual accounts of her childhood and adolescence which try to interpret the bare events, but none which approach the real reasons. When I met her again, six years later, she recalled our past meeting (for me it had occured only four hours previously) and, whilst she was most cordial and polite to me, I sensed that she had regretted those hours of soul-baring. I knew that she now refrained from talking about either her childhood or her religious beliefs and had only once – to a young reporter – discussed her emotional life. I sensed that she had aged considerably in the six year interval. We sat in her Boston apartment, overlooking the sprawling, spired city, drinking a dry white wine (a soya-wine that was surprisingly an improvement upon the natural product). Her personal robo-servant waited on us quietly and efficiently, the photocells of his eyes glowing a sudden bright red when I praised the wine.

"I sometimes think that we shall eventually produce a robot with far greater sensitivity that a man. A 'being' with aesthetic taste, with an ethical code and with supreme intellectual and physical attributes. It seems that *we* were created imperfect, but there is no reason why our own creations should mimic our views as well as our virtues."

As ever with Dr Susan Calvin, it was only when she talked of robots that her voice shed its habitual lack of colour and became injected with enthusiasm. Leaning her frail frame towards me in her seat, Dr Calvin talked at length about her mechanical charges, with a mother's fondness. On the walls of her apartment were hung holographs and complex design charts of various models, humanoid and non-humanoid. As she talked of them, the robo-servant brought each picture to her in turn, as if familiar with her routine. She explained:

"Robots are always topical. I have many visits from the press and the holovision people. Some come simply to find fault, others seem to be sympathetic, but they're only here to further some technological lie. Few of them really understand. Even in US Robots there are those who see our work only in terms of the immediate financial return – who ignore that we have a more significant role to play in the future of Man."

That evening spent in her company convinced me of the existence of a tender caring core to Susan Calvin. At 35 she already had the reputation of being a hardened career woman, of not suffering fools gladly and of being a perfectionist. An only child, her parents were still alive in 2017, though they were another of the topics she rarely spoke of.

Plate 3. *Dr Susan Calvin, aged 74, gazes fondly at Robbie, an early non-vocal robot. Behind her the massive Leviathan complex, belonging to US Robots Inc., continues production throughout the night. By 2056, when this hologram was taken, US Robots were exporting 128,000 androids per annum to the colonised outer planets.*

"These creatures are my family. They are orphans. Few other people *really* care about them. But if we *don't* care then, ultimately, we shall suffer for our neglect."

Beside her on the chair she clasped a loose-leafed manual, her own notes scattered amongst its up-dated, printed sheets. It was the famous HANDBOOK OF ROBOTICS, with its list of general principles and coded reference sources. Reprinted in book form every three years, only Dr Calvin and five of her senior colleagues had the constantly amended manual. I wondered if she could visualise that in five hundred years someone would pay three million credits at auction for that slender folder.

Forty-two years later I met her for the third time. In my disguise she did not recognise me, but welcomed me brusquely to her office in the giant US Robots complex in Philadelphia. She was no longer the chief robopsychologist of the Corporation. Two of her young protégés now divided the work between them, each backed by a team of specialists. She was the Corporation's "Grand Old Lady" now – retained for her astute advice and her immense experience. In her straight-backed chair she looked much smaller than I had remembered; a certain sign of her age. But her eyes displayed that same vitality and enthusiasm for her job that I had seen in the younger woman. She had no regrets about that. What she did regret was the bitterness of her struggle to break down Mankind's prejudice against the robots.

"It could have been easier. So many people could have helped so much. But they're all concerned only with their own *small* interests. So few of them actually had the vision to see the true potential of the robot."

I thought of Stephen Byerley, the robot who had lived as a man, and I thought of the Machines which now ran the delicate economy of the world. Susan Calvin had witnessed massive changes in the ways of the world and, as she had foreseen in that youthful essay, she had helped Man to adapt to those changes by providing him with a faithful instrument – a partner.

Behind her on the wall of her office was a holograph taken three years earlier. In it Dr Susan Calvin stood before the massive USR building, its cluster of sharp lights seeming to reflect the night sky. Moving away from her, towards the holo equipment, strode one of the earliest non-vocal models, an RB(n/v) as it was catalogued in the Karel Capek Museum of Robotics, but better known to her as 'Robbie'. As she talked to me I tried to fathom the meaning of her expression in that holograph as she gazed at that mute but magnificent machine. And perhaps there was only one conclusion I could come to: that it was love – mother love – for what she saw as a new and better breed.

In some universes Man and his Technology have achieved a degree of harmony: becoming partners and not antagonists. In Susan Calvin's universe such a balance had been reached, but, in the crucial manner in which all such matters are decided, it was Susan Calvin's individual effort that had created the necessary climate for that balance.

With the massive, light-littered bulk of the USR complex behind me, I shed my disguise and calmly stepped out of the air and into the flux between the universes.

The character of Susan Calvin has been portrayed by kind permission of Isaac Asimov, author of I, ROBOT and THE REST OF THE ROBOTS (published by Doubleday and Company, Inc.).

— T H E —
· ILLUSTRATED MAN ·

Back in the early part of Earth-Prime's Twentieth Century, if you were to travel about America, visiting the small town carnivals, you might well have come across the illustrated man. I met him in August 1946 in Wisconsin, where I guessed he might be – searching constantly for the old woman who, so long before, had covered his body with her fateful and fascinating tattoos. He asked me, as he must have asked so many others, if I knew where he could get a job, and, when I said no, he sat down beside me and – as I had hoped – began to talk about himself.

It was early morning when he began, and, as he talked, I learned more about him than I had ever gleaned from the old stories. I knew that in 1900 he had met an old woman ("a little, crazy old witch" he would constantly call her) whose sign had caught his eye. "Skin Illustration" it had read. He sat and told me the details of that all-night sitting, when his skin had become a tapestry of things to come.

He had always been a freak of sorts. When he was only six he was often mistaken for a young man in his early twenties. He was well-built and his face seemed cursed by fate to be forever ahead of its time. So, when he was twenty, people would mistake him for a man in his fifties. His mother – he didn't think even *she* knew who his father was – had kicked him out when he was twelve and he had toured the carnival circuit, moving from town to town, looking for something that he had never experienced: security. When he had broken his leg on his twentieth birthday it was just another example of his bad luck. Carnival owners knew him for it. He was the 'boy-man' who was forever at the centre of any mishap, the cause of any accident.

Perhaps it was the desire to change his fortunes that motivated him to seek out the old lady from her roadside sign. Propping his stick against her door, he had rapped loudly on the heavy brass knocker and then stepped back, standing on that quiet porch with his weight resting on his good left leg. In a few seconds the door had swung back and a woman, her hair tied up in a bun at the back of her neck, ushered him into the dim interior.

The little house was austerely furnished and its single downstairs room contained only two chairs and a curious box-mechanism. She waved him to sit in one of the high-backed chairs and sat across from him. For the first twenty minutes neither of them spoke, and he found that he was compelled by her gaze to remain silent. She was a delicately built yet compact woman, whose face seemed to flow in the uncertain light, preventing him from assessing her age. As if coming out of a trance, she went

across to him and took him by the hand, leading him to the strange box-mechanism which rested against the back wall. She sat him on a low stool, placing his right leg on a padded iron rest that extended from deep within the contraption. She had gently removed his shirt, exposing his broad chest and back, and then moved behind him to unsheath the tattooing needle from its leather arm.

He had witnessed little of the actual process of 'illustration'. What he had seen was the shadow of the old woman as she moved swiftly, furiously about her work. A dull red light suffused the long, low-ceilinged room, interspersed with vivid blue-white flashes of electric glare that left a sharp after-impression on his retina. For the first hour the stinging movements of the 'needles' were sharp pains that had set his nerves on edge, but after that his sensitivity was dulled. Throughout the evening she continued with her intricate task, turning him slowly on the revolving stool, covering every inch of his upper torso with the amazingly complex designs.

In the early hours he awoke from a light slumber, feeling a faint vibration beneath the surface of his skin. He was facing the machinery and, with a slight start of surprise, realised that the machine was like a large transparent vase, within which a strange mass of glowing red entrails writhed and heaved. It was as if the glass walls of the machine contained some living thing. From the crown of the apparatus a slender armature extended, at the end of which there were no needles but, instead, a fine blue flame that fanned delicately into a complicated arrangement of dancing, flickering sparks. As the flame passed across his skin, the dermal layer glowed and then seemed to cool to a dull red. Then, as it 'cooled' further, a spectacular design was revealed, etched in vivid colours that seemed to glow brighter and brighter as the seconds passed.

In the early dawn he had limped slowly from the house, his skin glowing as though he had been exposed overlong to the fierce summer sun. In the next town along the road he had hired a room in the best hotel and, with the door locked, had studied the old woman's handiwork in a full-length mirror. What he saw had, at that moment, pleased him more than anything had pleased him in his whole life. He felt that his luck *had*, at last, changed. There were about two dozen tiny scenes etched upon the surface of his skin; each of them as perfect as an old master in one of the East Coast galleries.

For five dollars he had bought himself a lifetime's occupation. Every carnival in the country would want to hire him as an attraction. That night, as he lay naked on his bed, he imagined the hoardings and the crowds, the queues at the flap of the booth to see 'The Illustrated Man'. But as he lay there the faint tingling of his skin became a violent scratching sensation and, as he looked on, the figures began to move, the scenes to change.

Plate 1. *The Illustrated Man, his body prematurely aged, is seen here during the all-night sitting when, as a twenty-year old, the crazy old woman and her machine traced the intricate patterns of futurity upon his skin. We have since identified the machine as an adaptation of the commonly used Flux-Probability Stabiliser: though it is not yet understood how the old woman managed to convey the Stabiliser's intricate properties to the Illustrated Man's skin.*

Plate 2. *The pictures on the Illustrated Man's chest were forever changing. Each night they would enact their own particular destinies. His skin acted as a receiver for all the tragedies of the universe, drawing together on its canvas scenes from the past and the future, from Earth and from other worlds. This photograph, taken by our invesigator without the Illustrated Man's knowledge, shows some of these scenarios. There is a noticeable pattern of guilt and retribution.*

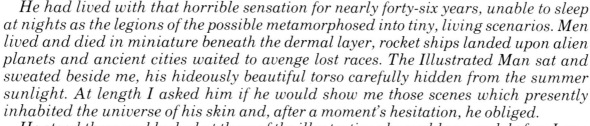

He had lived with that horrible sensation for nearly forty-six years, unable to sleep at nights as the legions of the possible metamorphosed into tiny, living scenarios. Men lived and died in miniature beneath the dermal layer, rocket ships landed upon alien planets and ancient cities waited to avenge lost races. The Illustrated Man sat and sweated beside me, his hideously beautiful torso carefully hidden from the summer sunlight. At length I asked him if he would show me those scenes which presently inhabited the universe of his skin and, after a moment's hesitation, he obliged.

He stood there and looked at those of the illustrations he could see, and, before I was drawn hypnotically into the various tiny scenes, I noticed that there was no trace of interest in his face. There was only disgust and a haunting despair.

The pictures were every bit as marvellous as I had expected. It was not as if they were actual pictures, but three-dimensional fragments of something real – something that had been momentarily frozen at a point where some great tragedy were about to occur. The Illustrated Man sighed and told me that he had never known any of the shifting stories to have a really happy ending.

"It's as if all the sorrows of the entire universe are being enacted one by one on the canvas of my body. Sometimes I notice one that seems to have reached a happy resolution, but always, without exception, it returns at some later stage. of its development, this time ending in tragedy. Yes, there's nothing to be seen here but isolation, desolation, betrayal, unhappiness and death."

There, on his torso, were the symbols of a grotesque cosmic carnival: the painted lures of the flesh; invasion fleets sailing outward into the void; the brutal mask of the android executioner, and a death's-head chained to a mockery of life. As night fell each scene in its turn would melt and flow, complete its destiny and be replaced.

"I once met Emma and Willy Fleet, you know – the dwarf and his wife. She believed he had tattooed her, and he similarly believed it. Emma was four hundred pounds plus. She came up to me at a carnival and introduced herself as The Illustrated Woman. But she was fortunate; it only brought her happiness. For me it is a continuous pain . . . a curse."

He had not aged since that day in 1900, neither had he ever been able to trace the crazed old woman who, with the help of her strange equipment, had damned him to walk the earth friendless and feared.

"You know, that old woman didn't say much to me. She said she could 'illustrate' me better than any tattooist ever had or ever could, and she said that she came from the future and was a time-traveller. Those two things only, she said. The first I now know for the truth, and so the second I have to accept too. Where or

Plate 3. At first the Illustrated Man found it easy to get employment and became a notable attraction at many major carnivals, drawing large crowds. He is pictured here in Hibbing, Minnesota, where, three days after this picture was taken, the Marquee was destroyed by fire, killing thirty nine people. Such incidents dogged him throughout the early years of the Twentieth Century, and eventually he found it difficult to get work, his potential employers becoming unwilling to take the risk.

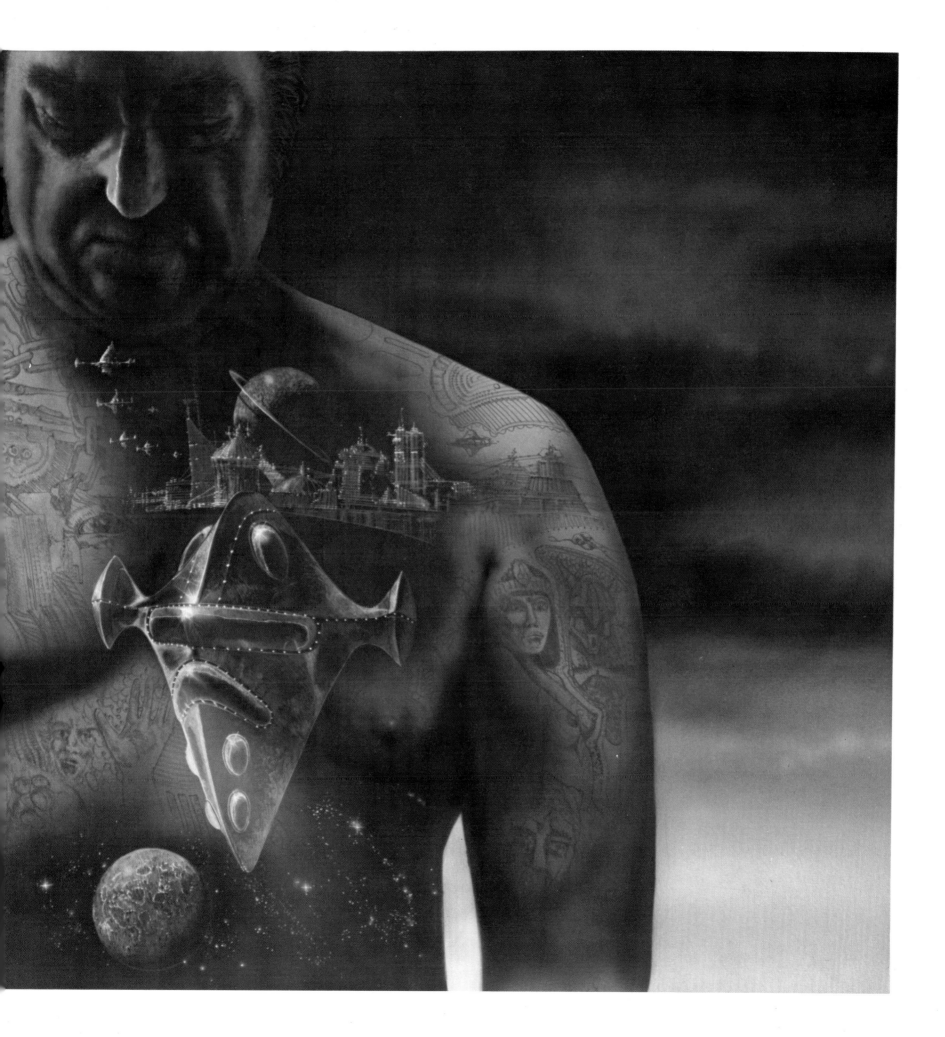

when she came from I never knew, but when I catch up with her I'll make her die horribly for what she's done to me, if it takes forever."

The day was waning and soon the shade of early evening would deepen into night. As he turned slowly I saw the small, empty space of skin on his right shoulder where, I knew, if I waited long enough I would witness my own death. I was not afraid. I had already seen my own death a dozen times and come to terms with it (as we all must who become students of Muir). Seeing me gazing at the spot, he warned me that I must not stay by him when the darkness fell and told me the story of the young man who had also listened to his tale. Like me he had sat and stared at the intricate designs and heard his quest to find and kill the old woman. Sleeping by him, heedless of his warning, he had woken to find The Illustrated Man at his throat, deep in the midst of the hallucinatory dreams he had when lacking sleep. Believing in his dream that the young man was really the future witch, he had slowly choked the life from him before waking from his vengeful nightmare. Remorse had not reversed the deed.

"So you must go and leave me on this cursèd road. I'll find her; I'm sure of it. Then I shall be able to rest. Perhaps with her death the pictures will fade and vanish and I will grow old and wither away with them. Ah, what a joy that would be."

I left him there, on the grassy bank of the road, placing a low hill between us before I sat and adopted the first attitude. As my outline faded I had one final vision of him, head bowed in fatalistic despair as I walked away, preparing for another night alone with his living pictures.

·SLIPPERY JIM DIGRIZ·

It was hard at first to know whether it was DiGriz I was talking to. Sitting across from him on the subterranean-intercontinental-connecting-tube I introduced myself as the Head of a large Multi-System Mining Corporation specialising in the excavation of rare gems such as the Procyon Opal. His interest was casual but definite. I had set myself up as another dupe for Slippery Jim DiGriz. ("James Bolivar DiGriz" his passport read, but that, like his physical features, was doubtlessly a product of his lively imagination.) Beside him, Angelina kept quiet. She behaved almost as though she were travelling alone and had never met DiGriz before that trip. She observed our conversation with the bland indifference of someone who was bored with the niceties of existence. But I knew that she, even more than DiGriz, would be remembering every word and storing every nuance of our discussion for future use. She was as attuned to DiGriz's plan as he, even though nothing more than the most covert of glances (scarcely noticeable – and one I would have missed had I been genuinely the man I was posing as) passed between them.

It was a two hour journey of some eighteen hundred kilometres. In the space of that rapid transit I had hired James DiGriz, Doctor of Palaeontology, specialising in the fossil-gems of the Procyon System. It was an impressive display. DiGriz took the slender outline of my fake explanation and, drawing on his eidetic store of knowledge (and his grasp of palaeontology was truely encyclopaedic), built up a credible new scheme for extracting the rare gems at a third of my extraction costs. All I needed was his expert advice and an initial capital investment of five million Yrrah (linked to the T. Ceti Nosirrah at a rate of 1.8776 to 1, he added, jotting a few figures down on a hand pad). By the end of the journey he had a signed contract (which Angelina kindly agreed to witness: putting her name as Clara P. Jobbernowl, a name that even DiGriz found hard to swallow) and an invitation to join me in four weeks on Procyon V.

There was a simple explanation for my complex ruse. Procyon V was indeed a mining planet owned by the company that I supposedly represented. I had disguised myself to appear identical to the Head of the

Corporation, and ensured that the gentleman I was impersonating was on his bi-annual three-month holiday. DiGriz, I knew, would check all the facts. He would have memorized my face to check against the official files (which he would gain unofficial access to). He would not come to Procyon V without assuring himself that it was he who was in control of the situation. But once on Procyon V I would have his undivided attention for four months if I wished. What he would not find from the files (because I had altered them, substituting false information) was that Procyon V was a small, airless planet with only one small mining community (under a Fullers Dome) that was visited by rocket only once every four months. It was as far out from Procyon's sun as Pluto is from Sol. Once there, DiGriz would have to stay.

Four weeks later Jim DiGriz arrived on Procyon V, with a young girl whom he introduced as Zina L. Blockhead. Through the full-body-disguise I noted that certain aspects of Angelina's former appearance protruded.

Within an hour DiGriz had realised he had been set up. It was, however, too late. The ship had gone. He confronted me in the bar, without Angelina, ordering us both drinks, and eyed me up and down with an expression which hovered between inquisitiveness and anger. However, when he finally understood that I was not one of Inskipp's 'Special Corps' agents keeping tabs on him, the look of anger faded and he gladly accepted a second drink. When I laid the case filled with old, unmarked bills open before him his quizzical expression changed to one of unfeigned surprise. (I could almost see the mental calculations – Ten million Yrrah, with a banker's note guaranteeing an exchange rate of 1.8725 against the Nosirrah. He was, it seemed, more interested in how I had attained the exceptional rate.) But even then I was far from certain that I had hooked him. Slippery Jim, as his name implied, was elusive. When he had raided the Nairb National Bank on Ssidla, a whole army of police robots had failed to prevent his escape. His disarming charm, his innate cunning and his unflinching courage when there was a pile of money to be made, had enabled him to escape in his one-man flypod then. I was far from sure that I had cornered him yet. Though I knew he was partial to life's luxuries, I was also conscious that it was the challenge that was of paramount importance to him. What worried me most was the possibility that what I asked of him was not to be bought for any sum. If that were so, then I would have the near-impossible task of tracking him down (never knowing his real name) amongst a thousand billion highly-similar male children on a hundred thousand extremely similar worlds. Fortunately he merely smiled and signalled the barman to bring us two more drinks. Then he began to talk about his childhood.

He was born on Duwirth, a planet that had been in the Union of Worlds for almost two millenia (another, popular account of the Stainless Steel Rats – Hamill's THE

WAINSCOT MEN – gives a markedly different place of origin for DiGriz). It was a world upon which a healthy body and a healthy mind were pre-programmed into every citizen on conception. In young Jim's case something had gone wrong. Genetic engineering and a fine-screening of all psychological traits had produced a bland, strictly conformist world: one which had nauseated the uniquely anti-social tendencies of the young DiGriz.

He finished his third akvavit and I called for another, asking the barman to bring us a box of his best cigars at the same time. I had attempted to anticipate DiGriz's requirements and, thus far, had succeeded perfectly. He was in a talkative mood, and when Angelina joined us she listened as attentively as I to a rare glimpse of the real Jim DiGriz (she confided to me later that even she had not heard any of it before).

Early childhood had at first been a depressing, miserable affair for the spirited child. Unprepared by his nurture to cope with the irrepressible desire within him to break the rules, he had fallen foul of the punishment-machines time after time. He had been an unwilling sufferer at first, but later he had developed a perverse desire to prove himself unaffected by the soothing voices of the psychological-rectifier and the numbing shocks of the personality-adjuster. The numerous treatments had sharpened his wits, enlarging an already precocious degree of cunning such that at the age of eight he was able to silence the whispering, wheedling voices with a few carefully-worded but paradoxical answers to its straightforward questions. With a few minor electrical adjustments he had turned the adjuster into an enjoyable experience – the 'punishment' becoming a shot of momentary ecstasy delivered direct to the pleasure-centre of the brain.

"But there was a lot that the environment taught me. Duwirth was planned and organised on the blueprint of a hundred thousand other worlds. By learning how to manipulate its social structures and overcome its limitations, I learned how to survive as an individual in a galaxy full of unfortunate half-men stifled at birth by a system that has to impose conformity in order to cope with the sheer numbers of humanity."

He sat back and drew at the large cigar. For a moment, his expression set in earnest concentration and with Angelina watchful beside him, I could imagine the two of them beneath the huge metropolis of Jerent, working against a tight deadline to deactivate the Ihici fighter-fleet before it could create havoc throughout the neighbouring star systems. Angelina, as ever, was dressed provocatively, looking all the while as if she were keeping some vast and potent power under a tight leash. I knew her pre-psych-treatment history of callous murder and sensed that – unlike DiGriz – in extreme circumstances her murderous traits might surface again from deep within her. But, for now, she smiled beneath her blue-black, short-cropped hair and listened to the muscular DiGriz as he talked of his adolescence.

He had travelled far in his teens, acquiring the rudiments of those basic skills which he was later to perfect: safe-cracking; forgery; confidence tricks; simple

Plate 1. *In this security-camera holoframe, Police humanoid robots are seen pursuing Slippery Jim DiGriz, after his daring raid on the Nairb National Bank of Saidla.*

Plate 2. *Angelina, discovering that she has 'killed' a cybernoid security guard.*

Plate 3. *DiGriz and Angelina work against time in the massive, womb-like hangars of Ihici to sabotage the sleek Gahadim thrust fighters and prevent the insemination of the nearby Galaxy*

robbery, and political manoeuvering. He had spent a single, frustrating year perfecting his knowledge of standard Union of Worlds Law, and throughout his extensive travelling had kept up his education – soaking up the raw facts of existence with an eye always open for the utilisation of some of those facts in a new confidence trick.

"Even then I never did the same thing twice. I would try to find new angles, new approaches. I would always diversify. I learned what made people tick – basic psychology, I guess – and then used it to manipulate them. Most of all I learned just how blind and stupid conformist government *is,* and what opportunities it allows the gifted individual to exploit it. Conformity breeds routines, and routines in turn breed an apathetic response to life. My sort of crime thrives on apathy."

DiGriz was thoroughly enjoying himself. With the closed suitcase resting on his lap, a cigar smouldering between his teeth and a fifth glass of akvavit in his hand, he seemed perfectly at ease. He illustrated how he had learned to survive with small, amusing anecdotes, and the hours in that never-closing bar passed swiftly. At last he came to the time when he had first met and fallen in love with the then-murderous Angelina.

He recalled the strange mixture of emotions he had experienced: the attraction he had felt for her physical beauty and the strong aversion for her indifference to the great suffering she caused all of those who stood in her way. She had even tried to kill him – and very nearly succeeded. He, in turn, had stymied her plan to steal a giant space-battleship and make herself Empress of a large portion of the Galaxy. As antagonists they had nearly put paid to each other, but as a team they were undeniably successful in their efforts to end the careers of the *real* criminal element in the Galaxy – the kind that maimed and killed for fun. It was ironical in Angelina's case, yet she too believed in what she was doing with the rational part of her mind. As a team they had a tentative agreement with the "Special Corps" – they went their own inimitable way until urgently needed on some task. It suited them both. Their way of bucking the system did little *real* harm and – as Inskipp had to agree – merely re-distributed the money supply.

DiGriz stubbed out his cigar, swigged back his drink and passed the case across to Angelina.

"Well, we must be going now. You've got what you wanted and I, at least, have enjoyed myself."

He paused and smiled at my expression of bemusement.

"I know the ships only call here every four months. That's why Angy and I landed here three weeks back with a pair of ships and left one for an emergency. We figured you had to have some strange angle, changing the official records the way you did. Anyway, it was nice recollecting the old days. I hope we have the pleasure of your company again, some day."

With that he took his leave. Angelina stayed for a while longer to talk with me, but then, when he returned to say all was ready for take-off, she leaned across and whispered a parting line of advice:

"Don't believe a word . . ."

Back in my dormicle I wondered how much of it had been true. Any of it? In any case, there would be no second chance to talk to Jim DiGriz. Clearing my mind, I began the Muir disciplines and slowly faded out of that particular existence . . .

·OSCAR GORDON·

I waited until there was a lapse in their conversation and then approached them. The dwarf noticed me first, bringing me to the attention of Gordon. Gordon pushed aside his coffee cup and beckoned me to sit across from him. He was a well-muscled man, without the slightest hint of flabbiness, and his alert brown eyes seemed to cut through my disguise. The late afternoon Paris sidewalk was busy with the tourist trade, and as I sat beneath the shade, the heat and noise of the August day diminished.

The dwarf was Rufo, grandson of Star, Empress of the twenty universes and wife of E.C. ("Easy") Gordon – a man better known as 'Scarface' or 'Oscar'. A Hero. Oscar listened to me patiently, nodding slowly as I finished. "Sure" he said, and then it was my turn to listen as he began to talk about all those things he had left out of his account of the journey down the Glory Road. As he talked I studied his gestures, watching the abrupt movements of the long pink scar at the bridge of his nose, a vivid gash against the tan of his face, and the casual, animal grace of his body as he emphasised his story. I had asked him to talk about his childhood; about the things that had made him become a Hero. He had laughed and then obliged.

He had been born in 1937 at a small US Marine training camp in Virginia, and at the age of 5 had moved to Boston while his father fought in Europe. The cold winters there had bred in him a longing for warm, exotic climates, and a permanent aversion to the bleak New England winter landscapes.

After his father's death he had lived for a while in Florida with his mother, where his childhood love of adventure stories had become a passion. After his school hours, and when he was not swimming off the beaches of Miami, he would curl up in a chair with the exploits of Captain John Carter, reading all of Burroughs' Mars books again and again, imagining himself teleported to an alien planet, triumphing against all odds through the skilful combination of brain and brawn. He had been a cub scout at the time and had been fortunate enough to find himself in a troop led by an eccentric French teacher, Andre Fournier, who had introduced him to the rudiments of fencing. As with so many physical activities he discovered he had a natural aptitude for the sport, and the combination of rigid exercise and exotic skill formed a necessary outlet for his highly active imagination.

Oscar never had the chance to know his father, and those early years were spent

trying to fill that gap in his life. They were also spent travelling from place to place with his mother, trying to avoid the spectre of destitution. Jenny, his mother, was a pretty brunette whose sense of humour was her shield against the world's assaults. As they travelled across the Deep South she kept up a running bureaucratic battle with the Veteran's Administration, attempting to have her son classified as a War Orphan – and thus eligible for substantial financial support – and not just as a surviving dependent. The financial hardships of his youth were crucial in helping to form the hard shell of self-reliance he began to depend upon. Each move meant a new school, a new environment to be coped with. He was frequently in fights – that is, until the resident school bullies realised that Evelyn Cyril Gordon was not by any means as soft as his name suggested.

Despite the irregular schooling, Oscar had an insatiable curiosity and his natural grasp of mathematics kept him in academic favour whilst his performances on the football field promised, for a long while, a career in the game. His instinctive pursuit of the female sex began when he was living in Georgia, and a timely move to California in his mid-teens brought him into a more congenial atmosphere for that pursuit. His mother had met and married a young airman, and the move to California coincided with the escalation of the Korean War and his step-father's posting to Germany. He was left more to his own resources and industriously worked nights at a liquor store, claiming a few extra years when his casual employers asked him his age.

Throughout those college years Oscar was living with his father's sister and her husband, scraping together enough pocket money to buy the pulp science fiction magazines – feeling the constant need to satisfy his appetite for adventure. But there was another appetite that seemed to overshadow those needs at that stage of his life: the need for security and stability. His relationships with the young women at his College were marred each and every time by the conflicting desires within him; he wanted the continual thrill of discovery but also the security of a steady date. It was a dilemma he was never to resolve – especially when it came to Star.

Whenever he approached the subject of Star he would pause thoughtfully, exhaling the smoke of his Chesterfield cigarettes, sitting back momentarily to reflect upon something far beyond anything one could see in this universe.

At one such moment I interrupted his reverie to ask him how he had felt on that first occasion when he had stood with Star and Rufo in the nearby universe of

Plate 1. *Oscar 'scarface' Gordon unsheaths his sword, the Lady Vivamus, for the very first time. Behind him the breathtaking scenery of Nevia, with the massive Valentine Range of mountains dominating the skyline, contrasts with the urban landscape of Nice from which he had stepped only moments before. Star, Empress of the Twenty Universes, and her nephew, the dwarf Rufo, watch him and wait for him to make his selection from Rufo's mobile armoury. The Lady Vivamus was, however, to become his inseparable companion on the Glory Road.*

Plate 2. *When Oscar and his party entered the Universe of Karth-Hokesh, they were met by a welcoming party of ur-men; hideous green-skinned creatures with the outward forms of men. The swirling sky that was not a sky made their emergence a nightmarish experience. In the fight with the guardians of the gate, Oscar was wounded in his left side by a thrust with a sawtooth-edged blade, although both Rufo and Star emerged from it unharmed.*

Nevia and chosen his sword, the Lady Vivamus, from amongst the extensive armoury contained in Rufo's magic folding box.

That instant was at the very beginning of the long adventure that was to end in the mile-high black Tower, recapturing the Egg of the Phoenix. For Oscar it had been a satisfying moment at the time. As he reflected upon it across the years, however, he now filtered that memory through the realisation that Star had *known* everything that he was then about to face . . . and had not warned him. He had been on several quests with Rufo since that time, but none of them had had the innocent satisfactions of that first challenge.

There was a wistful look to him as he admitted that that moment when he had first drawn and held the Lady Vivamus had been one of the most contented of his life. The physical presence nearby of his 'dream princess', the sensation of the sabre in his hand like another limb, and the prospect of the challenge of the unknown – those three things had acted upon him like a powerful stimulant, making his blood pound. When he had once lost the sword for a brief while (*Rufo grinned at that memory*) he had fought a whole band of grotesque giants with his bare hands to recover it.

Oscar frequently laughed at himself, though it seemed he did not invite others to do so. As he recalled the fantastic events of his various journeys down the Glory Road I sensed a modesty in his recollections. It was Rufo who would occasionally interrupt to give him credit where he had owned to none. The two of them drank brandy and often seemed to be talking more to themselves than to me, as if the Earth I was on were perhaps less real than those other places they talked of. There was only one topic upon which the two of them seemed a trifle reluctant to talk, and that was the raid on Karth-Hokesh. I coaxed Oscar gently, subtly towards the subject and eventually he came to it.

He had not been afraid for himself, merely of dying and losing Star. When they had come through the gate into the universe of Karth-Hokesh that fear had powered his sword arm. Amidst that tangle of hideous alien bodies, and beneath a glowering non-sky, they had saved each others' lives again and again.

The defenders of the gate were designed for a single purpose – to kill anything that materialized into the space they guarded. The smooth-skinned, ape-like creatures were only partly living: constructs of crude bone, muscle and flesh animated by the desire to kill any intruders.

Plate 3. *Oscar draws the dragon's fire as Rufo and Star aim arrows at the beast's vulnerable spots. The three adventurers had almost reached the cave wherein lay the gate that led to Karth-Hokesh when Oscar stumbled over a baby fire-breather and wakened its mother. The monster, akin to Earth's ancient tyrannosaurus rex, differed in that it had developed a mechanism whereby it could store, exhale and ignite swamp-gas, a highly inflammable form of methane. On this occasion the three overcame the brute.*

"We were too busy to be scared at the time. We had to kill those things or be killed by them. There was no time for niceties."

But that had not been the only occasion when the three of them had acted as a finely-tuned fighting machine. Needing to get to Karth-Hokesh, and running short of time, Star had taken them to a gate she had not planned to use. The approach to the gate was through wild country, infested with giant rats and equally-disproportionately-sized hogs. But, close to the cave where the gate lay, was a dense forest wherein were dragons; huge beasts like Earth's ancient *tyrannosaurus rex*. And those giant lizards could, at will, exhale a swamp gas – a form of methane – which burst into flame in the air before them.

As they approached in the darkness, the cave entrance came into sight. Oscar had thought he was home and safe, but then he had stumbled over a baby dragon. The mother, wakened by her young one's squealing, had attacked. Then, while the adult dragon's attention was firmly focused on chasing Oscar, Rufo and Star had planted arrows in its weak spots: beneath its tail and in both of its nostrils. Oscar had dodged about before it to draw its flame and, as its fire guttered and flickered out, he dashed in to thrust the *Lady Vivamus* through its eye and into its tiny brain.

"Dragons don't bother me so much these days. There are far worse things on the Glory Road; things to keep a much-travelled hero and a dwarf from feeling jaded."

And that is how I wish to remember them, sitting drinking beneath the shade on a bright Paris afternoon before setting out once again on the Glory Road; enjoying their momentary relaxation before the excitement of another adventure. Declining their invitation to join them on their journey, I left them then.

In a small hotel room to the south of the city I lay down on the bed and concentrated on the first of the attitudes . . .

· L E W I S   O R N E ·

There was one great difficulty in approaching Lewis Orne: how could I conceal who I was and my true origins from a man who was also a god? It was true that Orne had chosen to live as a man, but in doing so he had not forsaken his powers as a god. There was was no other option: he would have to know who I was and why I was there.

Even as I entered the matrix of time and space within which Orne existed, I sensed his immense *psi* powers. It was not that he welcomed me: it was more that he was aware of me and wanted me to know that he was aware.

I had landed on Marak in a one-man spacecraft, garbed as a priest of Mahmud, god of Orne's planet of Chargon. Even as I walked from the spaceport, I was conscious of how deeply everything was affected by Orne's mere presence on the planet. A vast aura of power seemed to emanate from him, weaving together the threads of chaos into the tight knit of order. There was no need to ask for directions: it was like being drawn to a blazing fire in a long, cold hall.

As I sat in the back of a hired flyer, giving an occasional curt instruction to the driver, I sensed that Orne's attention was momentarily focused upon me. Then, anticipating my desire for further knowledge of him, Orne placed an image in my mind, one that made me gasp involuntarily at its strength and clarity. It was as if I were Orne himself, lain within the crechepod in the I-A Medical Center.

There was the awareness in Orne that he was dead. His body no longer encased his vital soul: it was a hideous ruin that clung to life only in the most extreme definition of the word, kept from dissolution by the complex machinery of the pod. Elsewhere, Orne's thoughts ranged far and wide, dwelling upon his childhood on Chargon and the outdoor game he had once played with his tomboy sisters, Maddie and Laurie.

From his earliest conscious moments he had been aware of a strange dissatisfaction with his own way of life. His mother, Victoria, had coached him in the ways of guile, and taught him to make connections between facts which at first sight seemed to be unconnected. He sensed that there was some ulterior motive behind her constant schooling, but could never understand what it was. His father, the Member for Chargon, had died when he was six, and he had spent his formative years in a suffocating atmosphere of feminine domination. He had run away at seventeen to join the Federation Marines and had used that as a stepping stone to enter the

Rediscovery and Re-education service (the R & R) two years later.

I realised that Orne was amused, and sensed that the source of his amusement was his own youthful naivety. A voice formed gently in my mind:

> "Yes. I was a shallow creature then; led by some blind instinct to follow a path I did not understand. To become a god, it seems, one must first be manipulated – drawn along the narrow way to face oneself. Only then can one *become,* and, in becoming, learn to manipulate."

The flyer settled above a large quadrangular building, and I noticed that the driver was unconscious, as if in a trance. Orne had brought me directly to him. As I entered the west-facing door I heard the distinct metallic strains of a kaithra and knew that it was Orne's wife, Diana, playing the ancient Ayrb instrument. A young boy stared at me quizzically and then broke into a smile of welcome. I knew instinctively that the boy looked identical to the young Lewis Orne, and that the boy was Orne's son, Hal. I sat on the low, comfortable chair and, as I waited for Orne to join me, the images returned to my mind. It was as though my eyes were closed and the pictures formed upon the blooded orange of the inside of my eyelids. Faces swirled in towards the centre, and at the centre was the face of Lewis Orne, aware of all that had happened and was yet to happen in his universe.

It seemed that I re-lived every moment of Orne's life between the time he had joined R & R and the time he had met Umbo Stetson of the Investigation-Adjustment team (the I-A, as it was commonly known). I *became* Orne and experienced everything that his earlier, limited self had been through. I stood on the red dust world of Hamal, suspicious, my instincts aroused, and pressed the panic button. Then I joined the I-A under Stetson and was landed upon Gienah III. And throughout all of this I was aware of a nagging frustration that I could not identify the source of. I was conscious and yet unconscious of the fact that I, as Orne, was only partly alive: a two-dimensional creature in a three-dimensional universe.

I had experienced years of Orne's life in mere seconds. While my mind had been occupied, he had entered the room and now sat across from me. He was a stocky man of medium height, yet his movements were the fluid motions of a guru. The figure who faced me was Lewis Orne the man, not the god. This earthly Orne had chosen to blinker himself: to experience the infinite on a day-by-day basis. His short-cropped reddish hair crowned a face that was at once both impish and ruggedly handsome.

Plate 1 *The emaciated figure of Lewis Orne, his body left for dead by the women of Sheleb, comes to life in the crechepod of the I-A Medical Centre on Marak. Images of his past and future selves form in the field of his new-found awareness, as he follows the path of becoming a god. The scars of his ordeal on the matriarchal planet had not been easily erased and Orne had lain in coma for three months.*

Plate 2. *Lewis Orne was dropped onto the heavily-forested world of Giennah III where he was waylaid by Tanub, the High Path Chief of the Grazzi and his ape-like forces. Here Orne is seen at the forest's edge, the crystal spires of one of Giennah's two cities shimmering with a pale blue fire before him. Orne's intuitive mastery of this potentially war-like situation prevented the erasure of the non-humanoid Giennahn civilization.*

Faint scars remained on the left-hand side of his face and on his left arm – souvenirs of the ambush on Sheleb which had 'killed' him. The last thing in my mind before he had made me aware of him had been a memory of the moment when he had sat beside Tanub, the High Path Chief of the Grazzi, in his sky car on Gienah III.

"It was perhaps the single moment when I realised clearly that everything has its purpose and that the problems start when we try to control situations too stringently. Things must achieve a natural balance. Looking out at the crystal city of the Gienahns, I was awestruck by its primitive sophistication. The paradox of the crystal city was also the basic paradox of the universe."

He talked quietly, but with a powerful resonance that forced one to listen to all that he said with care. I had experienced his feeling of awe, and knew exactly why he had forced the I-A to accept a compromise and not destroy the aggressive Gienahns. The crystal city had been the second step on his path to godhood; the second of the three transcendent steps prophesised by the Chargonian Shriggar that manifested itself before the Abbod Halmyrach. Orne relaxed and I found myself once again experiencing all he had himself experienced as if I were he, re-living in a few moments everything that had happened between that moment on Gienah and the confrontation on the religious planet, Amel, with the spiritual leader of the whole Galactic League, the Abbod Halmyrach.

As Orne I sat in the chair during the 'test of the miracle and its two faces', conscious of the vast powers that were chained by religious disciplines on Amel. The wall in the large chamber shimmered and became translucent, and a giant reptilian Shriggar stepped out from it – a tangible product of my mind. I re-lived the deaths of my two young sisters and talked to Mahmud. I experienced something of what it is to become a god.

But Orne could take me no further along that path. I was back in the room again, and he was speaking softly to me.

"You have only the capability of experiencing so much, in spite of your disciplines. You can skip between the universes – something I cannot do, being tied inseparably to this, my *created* universe – but you cannot become a god. I tried to give you more, but your mind could not see what I attempted to show it. And so you are back here with me, Orne-the-man, on this far simpler plane of existence."

Plate 3. *On the religious planet, Amel, Lewis Orne had to undergo several dangerous ordeals to test his godhead. He is pictured here in the vast chamber where the test of the miracle and its two faces were undergone. A Chargonian Shriggar lizard is seen manifesting itself from the potent, iridescent web of power that shimmered at the barrier wall. From this ordeal Orne learnt the importance of judging no one but himself.*

He laughed and held out his hand to Diana, who had just entered the room. Young Hal was sitting at his feet, a volume of the "Rim Wars History" open before him.

"But this ungodly life has its more-than-adequate compensations, and so long as Diana does not try, like her Nathian mother did, to make me Commissioner of the Galactic League, I am quite content. We both still enjoy the occasional job of field-work for the I-A, dampening down the extremities of action before they become too explosive. But we enjoy a more quiet, homely life these days."

My attention had strayed to Hal. I had sensed that he was only pretending to study the ancient history text. And then I realised why I had become aware of this: I was experiencing a faint but definite exploratory trace of his mind in mine. Like his father, Hal possessed a strong psi power. In the seven-year old it was a diluted version of his father's all-embracing powers, but I sensed the potential in it — the capacity for expanding that power. Orne's voice sounded again, this time resonating in my mind alone.

"Hal's time will come and he too will create his own universe. He too will then be born anew of flesh and, like I before him, will struggle to become aware of what he once knew without effort. Gods *can* be born, yes. But they must also be *made*. Hal must suffer ignorance and death before he can claim the godhead."

I studied Orne's face as the words formed in my mind but could not penetrate beyond that enigmatic expression. As his voice faded his features melted into a pixie-like grin — an adult version of the smile Hal had given me in welcome. I realised that the room was now facing eastward and that a faint sea breeze blew in from across the sand-dunes. Orne had built his house in the middle of Marak's only desert: the only place of solitude on a densely-populated Administrative Capital. I took Orne's smile as a farewell gesture: a 'good luck' wish from a man who knew that luck played little part in the way the universe worked.

Smiling myself, I sat back and cleared my mind of all but the opening symbols of the Muir discipline. As they formed in my mind I felt Orne's awesome psi-field slip slowly into the web of darkness . . . and then disappear completely. I focused upon my next port of call and felt the flux of all times and all spaces whirl about me before coming again into focus.

·ESAU CAIRN·

In the rebuilt city of Thugra I sat in the Great Hall as the feast began. Strong ale was poured into a leather mug before me and a large platter of almost raw meat, seasoned with the bitter herbs of the hill regions, was passed along the line towards me. Beside me, wearing the single garment that all of the males wore, sat Esau Cairn. Amongst the dark-haired males he was immediately incongruous, being as smooth and hairless as a woman of the Guras. But there was no one amongst those fearless warriors who would have, for an instant, thought of comparing Cairn to the slender figures who moved silently between the tables, seeing to the needs of their menfolk. Cairn listened attentively as Ghor-the-Bear finished his story and then let his head fall back as he roared his hearty approval of the anecdote. Esau and Ghor were inseparable companions, and had been so since Esau had triumphed over the mammoth Kothan warrior when he had first arrived on Almuric, a fugitive from an Earth on which he had not fitted. I was Cairn's guest – the first fellow 'Man of Earth' he had entertained since he had fled the authorities of Earth. Amongst the crude-tempered warriors he stood out as a sensitive and intelligent man, as if he wore his skin inside as well as out. When he had united the Gura tribes he had sworn to bring culture to this planet, long deprived of it. One sign of his endeavours was a scribe, who sat just back from the table, a sober, beetle-browed fellow who declined the wine jug and spent his time noting down the fragments of boastful tale that circulated the long table. He was a member of the guild of scribes that Cairn had instigated with the help of his mate, Altha. She was in the kitchens, organising the preparation of the numerous dishes that were passed along the line of ravenous men. I drained my mug and called for more, the tiny de-toxication pill I had taken earlier breaking the rough brew down into its harmless constituents. I knew that, lacking the opportunity to show my skills at combat, these men would only accept me if I could demonstrate my proficiency at the ale jug. If I cheated a little, it was all part of my job. I noted how Ghor watched me drain a sixth mug, his battered old face cracking in a wide grin of appreciation as I shouted once again, and waited until a serving girl came to my shoulder with the great stitched skin full of ale.

All about the Hall large fires roared in their grates, throwing long shadows into the dim centre of the feast. As I sat and watched the animated faces, it was as if I sat at the bottom of a deep, illuminated pool and observed a strange, dream-like race of Neanderthals, led by a human demi-god, his body-muscles rippling in the amber light.

Suddenly, as if at a given signal, the harsh babble of their voices fell to a mild susurration, and the warriors across from me turned to face the open space before the largest of the Hall's fireplaces. From the darkness beyond the doorway a small, long-bodied Gura strode, coming almost to the table before he stopped and spread his arms wide before him. This was Jon-the-Hinde-sayer, singer of heroic exploits, voice of the remembered past of the Guras of Koth. His, until the coming of the scribes, had been the highest of Almuric's meagre arts. As the warriors listened, he sang the ancient tales of Koth, some of them as much as 15000 years old, coming, by leaps of centuries, to the most marvellous tale of all – the story of Esau Cairn, known as Ironhand. In awe, as though it were the first time they had heard the tale, the warriors listened. Behind me the scribe's pen scratched noisily across the paper as he translated this heroic story into a permanent form, to be stored, for the edification of future generations, in the Great Library of Khor.

Much of the minstrel's song was familiar to me. Esau's fight with the winged men, the Yagas, was a memorable incident from the Saga. He had just met Altha, wandering far from Koth, when the Yagas had swooped upon them and kidnapped the slender, unorthodox Gura woman. Though he had killed several of them and managed to pursue the Yagas back to their land of Yagg, he had eventually been captured and brought before Yasmeena, Queen of the Night and ruler of the city on the rock, Yugga. Esau had spoken to me earlier about the Yagas:

"They are an amoral, degenerate race. Theirs is the ultimate in self-gratification. There is no compassion in the city of Yugga. The poor Gura women who are taken there are used and then brutally discarded. Then, their carnal enjoyment of their Gura slaves completed, their evil lusts sated, the Yagas eat

Plate 1. *Esau 'Ironhand' Cairn had often, as a child, gone off on hunting expeditions with his father, Jeremiah. The old, rugged, mountain man is seen here looking out across the arid, sculpted landscape of his native Arizona. Esau was never to forget the wild freedom of that beautiful country where, in the cruel month of April, the sky would begin its long, unpitying burn. In that hostile, yet for Esau welcoming land, he had leaned the essentials of survival.*

Plate 2. *On the wide plain only miles from the town of Koth, Esau and Altha were attacked by the winged men, the Yagas, whose desire for female slaves was never sated. Though Esau battled with the evil, amoral men from Yugga, Altha was grabbed by the Yagas and taken to their city, where she was to become one of the maidservants of Yasmeena, Queen of the Night. Forcing one of the wounded Yagas to carry him, Cairn flew in pursuit of the kidnapped Altha.*

their victims. Surely if Hell exists anywhere it is, or was, in Yugga."

In the afternoon before the feast, which Esau had thrown in my honour, I had sat in his humble quarters while he had talked of those times before he came to Almuric – of the misery and bewilderment and the overwhelming frustration he had felt while still on the over-sophisticated Earth. As he told me this tale, Altha sat, quiescent, behind him. We picked at a bowl of berries as we conversed, speaking, out of courtesy to Altha, in the strange, gutteral tongue of Almuric.

As a boy he had idolized his father: been in awe of the self-containment of the man. Jeremiah Cairn had been a man of few words who had believed firmly in the creed of "actin', not taw'kin'" (*for a moment Esau broke into the broad accent of his birthplace*). In his mind he had retained a picture of his father, standing relaxed and in his element, outlined against the early morning sky of Utah. Esau could only have been four or five then, and, on the day he remembered so vividly, he had helped his father to track and kill a mountain lion. They had been out on a springtime hunting expedition north of the Colorado River. On that day all of the mountain craft his father had drilled into him suddenly made sense. That evening, as they sat and watched the blood-red glow of sunset that starkly silhouetted the striated desert mountains, his father had told him about the time when he, in his turn, had first been on a hunt with *his* father. Sitting there in the muted glow of the small campfire, the smell of roasting cat and burning spruce branches rich in the evening air, he had watched in wonder as the sun died and the sky grew black in mourning. He had wondered if his son, in years to come, would have this same marvellous experience.

Esau had laughed and patted Altha's slightly swollen belly, a look of joy brightening his eyes.

"If it's a boy, we shall call him Jeremiah, and I shall teach him those arts my father taught me. But here, on Almuric, he will be truly free. He'll have more than the handful of years of happiness that I had on Earth. And though he'll not see the grandeur of the Canyon, he'll have the marvels of Almuric instead – the tall, deserted towers of the black citadel, Yugga, and the mighty Girdle that encircles this planet."

Even as he recalled the marvels of his new, chosen world, he grew agitated, and the tone of his voice suggested that he was about to recollect some far less pleasant memories.

He had been raised in an austere Arizona mountain community early in the second decade of the Twentieth Century (*even his school records are vague about his date of birth*). From his mother, Lucy, he had learned to read and write, something

Plate 3. *The huge black, basalt-like rock upon which the city of Yugga was built, rises sheer out of the River Yogh. The city had perhaps stood on the summit of the rock, Yuthla, for several hundred thousand years, spreading its reign of terror throughout Almuric. At its base, the blue people, the Akki, lived in their town of Akka, paying obeisance to Yasmeena. It was against the might of Yugga that Esau Cairn led 9000 Gura warriors.*

Plate 4. *The giant, slug-like sandworm known to the Yagas as the Ultimate Horror, breaks out of its dome, freed by Yasmeena as her sadistic empire crumbles. Esau, having just freed Altha, faces the blind, mindless fury of the giant beast, unafraid and, as always, vibrant with fierce life. In their sudden and climactic encounter both man and monster fell from the huge city on the rock, landing in the river Yogh. Esau alone survived this dramatic and unlikely denouement.*

which prepared him for the move to Utah, prior to February 1919 when the Grand Canyon National Park had opened and their small township was disbanded. He began his schooling later in that year, at first impressing his school teachers with his ability to grasp quickly the essentials of his education – rare in a mountain boy, they had said – and his school friends with his physical prowess.

The school activity he had loved best, however, was running. On the small cinder track of the local sports-centre he was able to shrug off all his normal inhibitions and surrender himself to the pure physical joy of competition. Yet as he grew older and stronger things soured. He was constantly in trouble. His temper was virulent and, not always conscious of his own strength, he frequently snapped the bone of a friend who had, for a moment, forgotten the mountain boy's quickly-raised temper and made fun of his thick accent. Parents, naturally, had complained. Esau, whose instinctive inclination was to instantly forget a grudge and get on with living, was at first puzzled by the hostility his honest, but aggressive nature provoked. Later he learned to subdue his natural vitality – to keep it for the sports field – in his College days managed to avoid his earlier difficulties. But to do so he had had to learn to accept the ill-natured insults of the petty criminal element he encountered more and more as he grew older. His rough looks and harsh accent disbarred him from more congenial company. He was constantly judged without trial and he learned to live with that injustice. But, for all the time he was on Earth, he never grew to like it. It festered inside him and, like some cankerous growth, eventually burst wide open in the blind killing of a gangland boss who had pushed him too far.

Esau had paused in his tale, a moment of sudden realisation etching a broad smile upon his rugged features.

"It occurs to me that you might compare my old frustration to that of the Ultimate Horror, trapped in its dome by the Yaga Queen, Yasmeena. All of that ferocious energy contained within unnatural boundaries."

I remember his words clearly as I sat by him in the Great Hall. Jon-the-Hinde-sayer had reached the point in the saga when Esau Ironhand had freed Altha and, with the Yagas certain of defeat, Yasmeena had freed the giant dust-worm from its dome. The story was much embellished from its original form, though Esau's brave contest against the towering, mindless monster had been astonishing enough. The Gura minstrel came to the end of his tale and, after a moment's rapt silence, was rewarded with a hearty roar of applause from the warriors.

Much later I stood alone with Esau Cairn in the tall grass of the plain, beyond reconstructed Thugra's walls. Holding both my hands in friendship, he smiled and wished me well on my travels. I had told him that, like he before me, I had crossed the unimaginable gulf of space between Earth and Almuric without a vehicle. He had wished to witness my departure and, in response to his unstinting hospitality, I had agreed.

We parted hands and he stepped back, wishing me farewell in the tongues of Earth and Almuric as my outline grew faint against the dawn sky and shimmered into nothingness.

· BEOWULF SHAEFFER ·

I rested on the inoperative travel couch in the Camelot Bar waiting for Shaeffer to arrive, sipping at a cool glass of Taittinger Comtes de Champagnes '67, the slender bottle in an ice bucket on the table by my side. I had found the 1.78 gravities of Jinx oppressive out in the street, but here in the Bar it was a pleasant one gravity, Earth Standard. I distracted myself by studying a frieze on the far wall of the bar which depicted a group of bizarre-looking aliens, each engaged in an action typical of its species. There was an orange-furred Kzinti warrior in combat stance next to a creature that looked like a three-legged centaur without a head and with slender, serpentine arms – a Pierson's Puppeteer. A massive kdatlyno, built like a monster from Earth's nightmare distant past, all claws and horns, worked at a delicate touch sculpture, and a Grog stood immobile and conical, doing, or so it seemed, absolutely nothing. Grogs were possessed of great telepathic powers. Its expression was inscrutable mainly because it did not have one;something it had shed, like its arms, legs and external sensory organs in a billion-year devolutionary process. Around the border of thecomposition was a procession of Bandersnatchi, the sentient giant white slugs of the ocean shorelines of Jinx, linked mouth to tail in a dance that seemed to represent pure hunger. I was trying to figure out why the Puppeteer was partially erased when Shaeffer entered the bar.

The crashlander (the term for a native of We Made It, chief planet of Procyon and the place where General Products make their hulls) had shed his travel couch at the door and walked with apparent delight into the more comfortable gravity of the bar. He would have preferred it at six-tenths gravity, I was certain. He was a startlingly pale figure, as thin as the slender, fluted pillars of the bar, and outrageously tall – in excess of seven feet. When he sat down opposite me, stretching his long legs before him, I studied his albino features. With We Made It's 1500- mile an hour seasonal winds, the crashlanders lived underground, and it seemed that even though he now lived on Earth, he was still indifferent to the sun. Despite the tannin-secretion pills he took, his skin was still an almost translucent layer pulled tightly over a fragile framework of bones. A fine tracery of veins was visible through his skin and his eyes at

first seemed lifeless, but when he stretched out his hand to me and laughed, introducing himself, a faint red glow was noticeable in his pupils and at the tips of his ears, a sign of his embarrassment. It had cost me a million stars to lure him away from Earth and his wife, Sharrol. He was as curious about me as I was about him. But he did not come to the point immediately; he must have realised that my initial quizzical expression had to do with the frieze and the partially erased Puppeteer.

"It's meant to represent the gradual withdrawal of the Puppeteers from this galaxy. Ever since I discovered that the Galaxy Core was turning super-nova they've been hurrying to get as far away as possible. Cowards first and businessmen second, the puppeteers."

His voice was a soft, melodious alto, rather unexpected, though not without its charms after the harsh flatlander bellow that was to be heard elsewhere in the bar, or the Jinxian deep bass, bestial and sometimes almost inaudible. In his way he seemed more alien than the bizarre creatures of the frieze. I understood suddenly the title of the piece: "The less-alien aliens". Beowulf Shaeffer had broken the ice between us, and I encouraged him to talk about his encounters with the puppeteers, and he began to tell me about his first meeting with the president of General Products in a drug-store on We Made It.

He had never discovered the puppeteer's name – except for the rare ones (such as the insane Nessus, the *courageous* puppeteer) they never volunteered such information. He had simply been offered a large sum of money to do a very dangerous job and, to ensure that he had no alternative, the puppeteer had threatened to reveal Shaeffer's dire economic situation to the authorities if he did not volunteer. The puppeteer had taken him by displacement booth to the roof of the General Products building and shown him the No.2 GP Hull about which he was to design his own ship.

He had already written up that adventure with the neutron star ("had it ghost written," I corrected him) and had done likewise with several of his other unwilling brushes with danger. I was familiar with most of what he told me, and coaxed him to talk of his time as a space pilot with the Nakamura Line and, before that, as a young recruit to the crashlander marines in the fourth (and final) Man-Kzin War. He looked surprised when I asked him about his part in that war.

"Even Sharrol doesn't know I was in that! Finagle! If she realised how *old* it makes me!"

Plate 1. *Up on the roof of the General Products Building on We Made It, Beowulf Schaeffer is shown the badly damaged craft in which a husband and wife team had been killed when investigating a Neutron Star. The Pierson's Puppeteer, General Manager of GP, offers Shaeffer one million stars if he will design his own ship and fly to the Neutron Star to ascertain what strange and powerful force could penetrate a GP Hull. Beowulf reluctantly accepted.*

It seemed that the indolent, spendthrift Shaeffer was not averse to lying about his age. I had checked up on his origins in the Records section of the Institute of Knowledge, which houses the 'Galactic Census' (taking a few minutes, while I was there, to study the kdatlyno touch-sculptor Lloobee's composition "Heroes", which has the strange, attenuated face of Shaeffer as its centre-piece; warm and gently pulsing when I applied a gentle pressure with my fingertips). Shaeffer was, in fact, born in 2543. The year in which I had chosen to meet him was 2813. He was 270 years old. It explained something of his ability to get through vast sums of money in short spans of time. He obviously used boosterspice, the highly expensive, Jinxian-developed longevity drug, to maintain his youthful appearance. It also explained why he so readily answered my summons to Jinx, even when it meant leaving Sharrol for at least a month.

"You would have thought the Kzin would have known better. They'd lost three wars because they weren't ready to fight them, and the fourth time out they were about as poorly equipped as an invasion force could possibly be! There were only two of our ships waiting for them when they came sailing into Eridani making for Earth, but we turned most of them around and only had to mop up a few of the Kzin who had opted to land and rough-up the small colony on the fourth planet. It was in that operation that I found myself in a hand-to-hand combat situation with a full-grown Kzinti warrior."

It was not modesty that kept Shaeffer from milking the tale for all it was worth, but a strange kind of humanity. He had been armed with a power-axe, the Kzin with a simple *Wtsai* blade. The outcome had been obvious: Shaeffer had butchered the courageous but unprepared Kzin, and he was far from proud of the fact. From what I knew of Shaeffer I realised that he was devious and elusive, but – apart from a desire to cheat large corporations and governments – he was essentially honest. He had not remained a soldier for long: his temperament had been unsuited to the rigorous disciplines of marine life. He was basically lethargic and did not like to use either his physical prowess or his substantial intellect unless it were to save his skin in an extreme emergency. Fortunately, on the five or six occasions when it had proved necessary, his innate talents had seen him through. In another Age he would have been labelled an anarchist in his views. He liked to be his own boss, to do things his own way and, whenever the opportunity arose, he liked to throw a spanner in the works. For example, he had enjoyed paying back the puppeteers for sending him to the Galaxy's Core by frightening them with the news that the Galaxy was exploding.

From time to time he would pause and swig at the long, cool glass of Tzlotz Beer before him. The glass was attached by a narrow flex to the table and re-filled itself the

Plate 2. *Beowulf, in full Krieger armour and wielding a power-axe, comes face to face with a Kzinti warrior who is armed with only a razor-sharp Wtsai knife. The kzin had attacked the Eridani system during the Fourth Man-Kzin War and found themselves unprepared to fight the technologically superior, if numerically inferior, crashlander forces from We Made It. Shaeffer easily disposed of his opponent, though for years afterwards he was deeply ashamed of this encounter.*

Plate 3. *Beneath the renovated Santa Monica Freeway, Beowulf looks on in bemusement as his best friend, Greg 'Elephant' Patton and his girlfriend, Sharrol, discuss Elephant's proposed navigation of the ancient highway. In his turquoise hot-rod, nicknamed "Roadhouse Blues", Elephant risked his life, racing against a dozen other rich 'maniacs' (as Beowulf called them). The delapidated condition of the highways despite constant and expensive repairs is evident in this picture.*

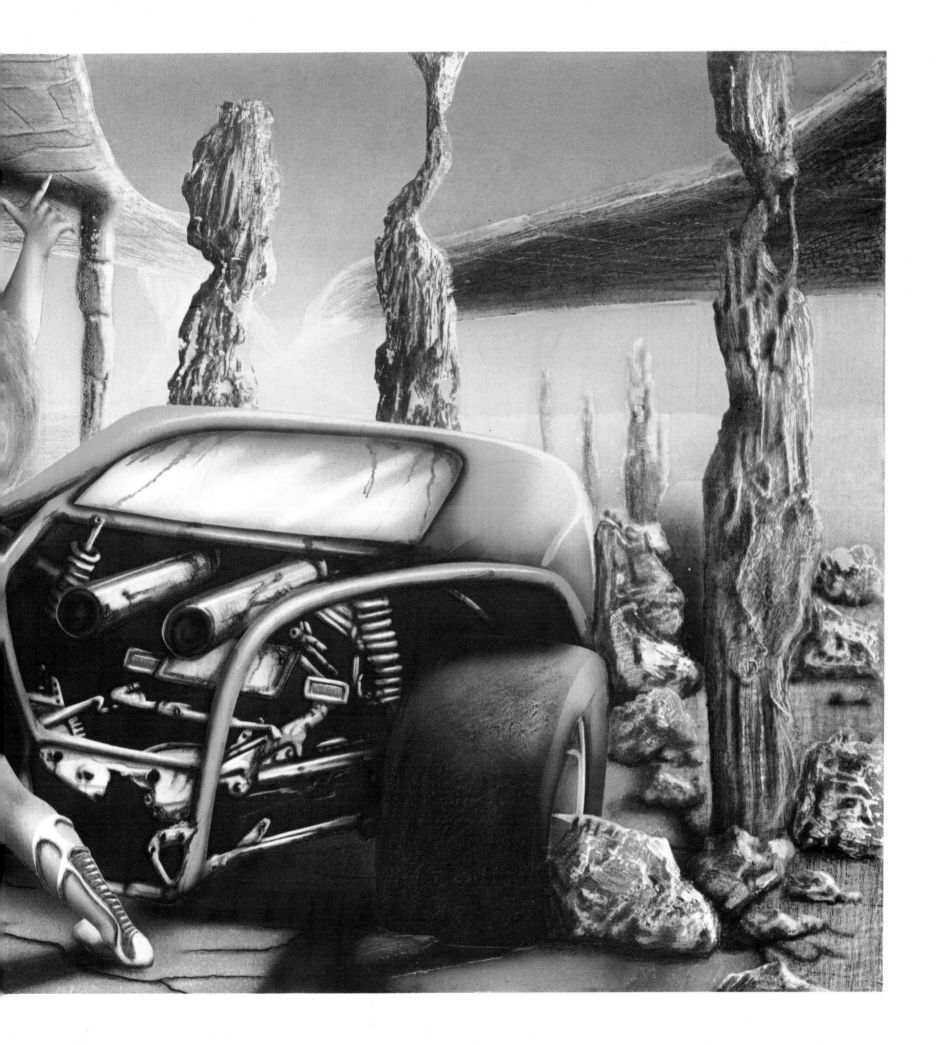

instant it was replaced on the smooth, jderwood surface.

"I learned how to fly a hyperdrive ship just as soon as I could. As a teenager I was fascinated by the prospect of being a space pilot. In the afternoons after school I would catch a walkway to Crashlanding Port and watch as the ships came in and the off-worlders unloaded their cargoes."

He had left the warrens of We Made It at seventeen. When he had returned, eighteen years and one Man-Kzin War later, it was to discover that both of his parents were dead, victims of a land-subsidence in the midst of a near 1700-mile-an-hour storm that was one of the worst recorded in We Made It's history. It had left a blank in his life that had not been filled until he had met Sharrol more than one hundred years later. She had first of all stolen his wallet and then, in what had been probably the greatest single coincidence of Beowulf Shaeffer's incident-packed long life, she had met up with him again at his good friend, Elephant's house. There, she had quickly stolen his heart.

'Elephant' was the nickname of the absurdly rich Gregory Palton, owner of General Products and half of Known Space. Shaeffer had, I knew, spent some time at his luxury home on the side of a cliff in the Rocky Mountains: an oasis of solitude on a world of eighteen billion people. At a dinner Shaeffer had been to with Elephant and the girls, he had gone as his natural albino self for the first time in many years. I knew that because of Earth's overpopulation problems the Fertility Laws banned all albinos from fathering children. There were no such restrictions elsewhere in Known Space, but Sharrol was unable to travel in Space. It had caused Shaeffer two years of heartbreak. Sharrol had had the children Shaeffer could not give her by his best friend, Carlos Wu. Now they were being brought up as Beowulf Shaeffer's children. But if he was still bitter about it, it did not show, and he was dressed as his natural albino self as he sat in the Camelot Bar with me, his snow-white hair almost shoulder length. He was talking about those early days with Sharrol and Elephant, and the time when they had watched the groundcars racing on the Santa Monica Freeway, one of the only two stretches of the highway network to have been maintained after the collapse of the groundcar economy.

"We went back there, Sharrol, Elephant and I. And Elephant took out his racer – a frail, ultramarine thing that looked all the while as if it would fall apart before he could complete the course. But Elephant held it all together and came in first. Crazy, those flatlanders!"

His irises glowed with a slight effusion of red, as if he were embarrassed by his own momentary wistfulness. Boosterspice would guarantee him a long life yet, and he showed no sign of tiring of it. When we had said our farewells and I was back in my room (thankful for the gravity-generators) I was tempted to see how it all turned out for Shaeffer. It would be peaceful, but anti-climatic. Nothing that followed could match what had gone before for excitement. I decided to leave it at that. Perhaps some student after me would, from curiosity, trace Shaeffer's life to its end.

Closing my eyes I pushed away from the matrix of Known Space and focused upon the next configuration of probabilities . . .

·WINSTON SMITH·

The blue overalls felt uncomfortable as I walked towards the huge, white pyramidal building. The surly ape-faced guards became more attentive as I approached and one of them, his black leather uniform reeking of animal sweat, stopped me with a curt request for my papers. As soon as he saw the special document with the initials of bb appended to the bottom of the second sheet he became suddenly servile – a cur to be kicked or treated as I willed. I passed him quickly, pitying him. Paranoia was in the very air I breathed. The year was 1984 and I was walking up the steps into Miniluv, the Ministry of Love.

Doors opened for me, an office was cleared for my use, files and tapes were brought before me at my request. Simple forgery and manipulation of a crude records system had made me a member of the Enclave, the core of the Inner Party and a personal adviser of Big Brother. The files were of a party member who had betrayed his trust and had had to be taught his duty of love to Big Brother. I opened the first file and removed the black and white photograph from its plastic folder. Winston Smith. His expression was that bland look of sheepish obedience that I would find in a hundred thousand other similar files. Under fair hair his skin looked dried and roughened. He had been 37 when it was taken. He looked ten or fifteen years older. There was nothing of the rebel in his manner, no sign of the deep-rooted intellectual dissatisfaction I knew he felt. Yet the picture was true to life – an expression of the instinctive fear that cowered him every minute of his adult life.

The contents of the first file were sealed; marked "Inner Party Eyes Only". I broke the seal, extracted the slender sheets of rough paper and began to read of Smith's childhood.

Winston Smith had been born in February 1945, son of William and Julia Smith. It had been the year before the revolution and his father had played a prominent part in setting up the workers' commune in his native Battersea (*now Section 14 of Airstrip One*). Winston had been brought up in the creche, learning the doctrines of the Party from the outset. Things had not been so rigorous or orthodox then, however, and the economy had not been switched totally to a War footing, so the young boy had sampled some of the then-present luxuries of Pre-War times which

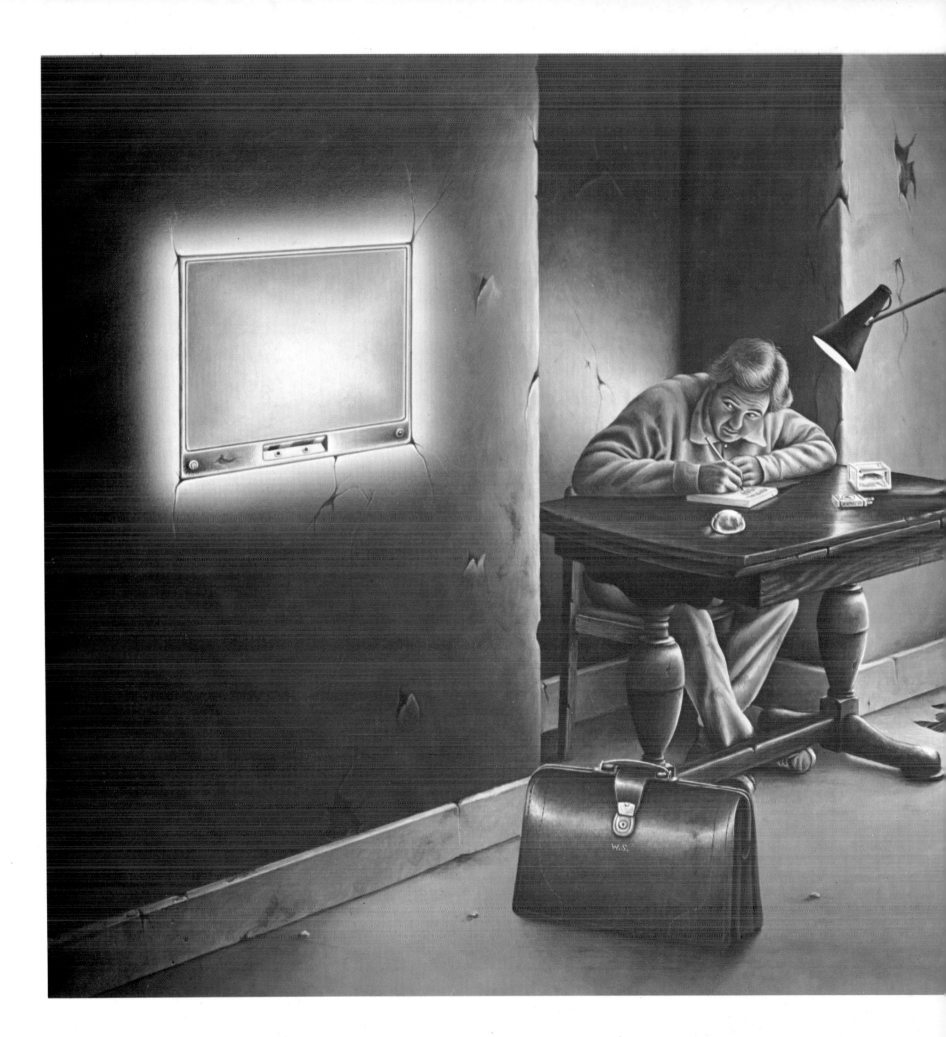

had been shared out amongst Party members. Things had soured rapidly in the early fifties with the first of the big purges when English Socialism had become Ingsoc and the three commandments of the Party (*to be seen engraved in the stone of the four Ministries*) had been laid down.

It was possible that Winston Smith had had a happy childhood. The records did not cater for such life-criteria in its information, so it was hard to tell. The Wars with Eastasia and Eurasia had drained the economy and ruined the towns. Life had become bleak. It became bleaker for Smith when his parents disappeared in the second of the Party's purges in 1956. He enrolled for the mandatory military service in 1961, a week after his sixteenth birthday, but the armed forces of Oceania found him unfit for active service. He spent four years in the Ministry of Army Records (*later incorporated into Minipax, the Ministry of Peace*) and showed a natural aptitude for the work. At 20 he passed the statutory exams for admission to the Party (*no longer part of the chain of recruitment*) and became a card-holding member. With this 'success' he was given his discharge papers from the Army and started within a week at his new job. In 1965, the Ministry of Truth was the only one of the four Ministries which was in its final, perfected form. It was not then housed in its imposing building, but scattered across Airstrip One in several smaller buildings. Winston Smith had been engaged to work as a junior pamphleteer, correcting the copy on party handouts and posters. Ironically, it was he who had, one Spring day in 1967, written the copy for the poster that could now be seen everywhere in the streets: the dark-haired, moustached face in its mid-forties which gazed out from its bright orange background. The suggested copy had read "The Party is keeping an eye on You" and Smith had abbreviated and personalised it to "Big Brother Is Watching You". Like so many of the jobs he did, it was soon forgotten. Memory was a malleable thing in this world.

The job in Pamphlets Department had led to a promotion into the Records Department of Minitrue, and a move, in 1969, to the new building a kilometre from where Smith lived in Victory Mansions. He had quickly adapted to the new work and had found that he was given work of the utmost importance to do. His job entailed the alteration of documentation to eradicate the Party's faults (*the file euphemistically called this "rectification of typographical errata", in what was a curiously non-Newspeak manner*). He re-wrote newspaper articles, altering the Past to comply with the needs of the Party. Throughout his time at Minitrue he had been a loyal servant of the Party, doing his job effectively and efficiently, joining in at the Two Minutes Hate sessions without a qualm. Yet this was also the man who had blatantly flouted the Party's most sacrosanct rules about sexual behaviour among

Plate 1. *In this collage of photographic impressions from the Inner Party's file on '6079 Smith (Winston)', Smith is shown in the niche where he wrote his secret and illicit diary, hidden from the probing eye of the Party's viewscreen. Through the window of his seventh storey apartment can be glimpsed the familiar, orange poster of Big Brother, with its paranoid slogan. In Andrew Muir's study of this probability world,* Two Dystopian Visions *(G82 Press; AD 31980) he notes Smith's major role in articulating the innermost thoughts of a typical Party worker, thereby creating the fear-mechanism by which the Party maintained its nine-thousand year rule. To the right of the picture can be seen Smith's work cubicle (superimposed here) with its Speakwrite, pneumatic tube and memory-hole. The delapidated condition of all non-functional equipment is noticeable.*

Party members. I wanted to try to trace some sign of this rebellion in his manner *before* he had started his illicit diary, and *before* he had met the dark-haired, anarchic Julia. Smith, I knew, had felt that the Party had eroded the outlines of his character until his past was a blurred, amorphous thing. But here, in the Inner Party records, was the crystalline shape of his past life, sharp in every detail. The private life of 6079 Smith W. was here preserved with the utmost lucidity. There was a good reason for it: he had, for a long time before his arrest, been considered Inner Party material.

From the files I moved to the Telescreen video records. For several hours I watched Smith in every aspect of his monotonous routine. I studied him as he partook in the early morning physical jerks, Smith wearing the standard expression of grim enjoyment, and later I observed him at his work. He sat unexpressively in his cubicle, intoning into the speakwrite in a clear, steady voice the day's few minor rectifications. I watched him in the canteen as he uncomplainingly ate the pinkish-grey stew and gulped down the oily Victory gin, the mask of earnest duty never slipping for a moment. There was no sign in all of this that this man could have suffered so greatly from intellectual and sexual frustration and not have shown it. There were minor displays of irritation, but they could quite readily be put down to the physical discomfort of his varicose ulcer.

There was nothing in the Miniluv records that might, before the event, have thrown suspicion upon 6079 Smith W. I had anticipated that it might be so and, under the guise of being a repairman (itself rare enough in these delapidated days) had planted my own untraceable, micro-miniaturised scanning device. The thought of using such a device was rather odious to me, yet it was essential for my purposes to establish the expression Smith had worn when he had sat in his alcove, the diary before him on the desk out of range of the telescreens. I removed the small, flimsy disc from the top pocket of my overalls and placed it on the smooth desk top before me. Touching it with the special stylus, I activated the disc. From the desk's surface rose a hologram of an apparently solid but miniaturised scene.

Smith sat rigidly at the desk, his pen resting upon the first page of the quarto-sized notebook. His expression was furtive, guilt-ridden. He seemed thoroughly conscious of the end this single act of rebellion would lead him to (indeed, his action in purchasing the book from Charrington's shop had instigated the Thought Police enquiry). A foreknowledge of doom was there already in his eyes. On the page before him was written the date: "April 4th, 1984."

I touched the centre of the disc and the interior of his seventh-storey room diminished and then disappeared altogether, to be replaced by another, earlier scene,

Plate 2. *A hidden spy-camera captures Winston Smith's momentary bewilderment as a Miniluv patrol helicopter lands near to him as he makes his way home from the huge, white pyramidal building of the Ministry of Truth, Minitrue, where he was employed. During these, the early days of Big Brother's nine-thousand-year rule, signs of the imminent First Economic Collapse (which led to the union of Oceania and Eurasia into WEST) are clear. Note the litter-strewn streets and the boarded-up windows. Even so, this scene is quite pleasant when contrasted with the bleak efficiency and neat austerity of the so-called Second Age of Revolution, when the proletariat were eradicated and the war with EAST became fully computerised. (Information courtesy of The Society For Ingsoc Studies Journal, Spring 31453: G82 Central Computer Index).*

taken in Brotherhood Walk, a street Smith always walked down on his way home from Minitrue.

A police patrol helicopter swooped down and landed on a vacant lot next to where Smith was walking. Smith stepped back in surprise and then stood meekly to attention as a black-uniformed guard questioned him brusquely. A telescreen had, for some unknown reason, blacked out. Smith, in the vicinity when it had happened, was a suspect. While the guard held on to Smith, his partner checked the screen and found it had been obscured by a wind-blown sheet of paper. The streets were strewn with such. It was only when the guards had gone that Smith allowed himself the faintest smile of irony. The offending paper had been part of a poster of Big Brother.

The look of doom and the faint smile were the only signs I had been able to trace of the human being behind the mask. Since his childhood he had been strictly orthodox in his outward activities. Admittedly, he had never been a zealot, but he had been a conscientious, unquestioning Party worker. His marriage to Katherine had failed, it was true, but that also was not uncommon. The only true failure in 1984 was to the Party.

I let the disc play itself out while I looked through the final two documents on the desk before me. The first was a quarto-sized notebook with a marbled cover and a red back – Smith's diary. I glanced through the untidy entries and noted the unpunctuated elegance of his later writings. It was all of him, really, that remained – all that had survived. The second document was the book he had read from to Julia the evening before his arrest: Emmanuel Goldstein's "The Theory and Practice of Oligarchical Collectivism". Like all else he had encountered in this fanatical world, it too was 'unreal' (and I realised suddenly that this was what the ancients meant by 'fiction'). They were both tragic texts in their own manner. Pushing them aside (knowing that, in time, they would be disposed of down the memory-hole with every other trace of Smith's existence) I summoned an assistant and asked to have the latest screening of Smith. Within a minute I was witness to a sad scene.

The almost unrecognisable figure with his bald pink scalp and his coarse features sat at his table in the Chestnut Tree Cafe, totally engrossed in the news from a blaring telescreen. A waiter hovered nearby, ready to top up his Victory Gin. A chessboard and a copy of The Times rested on the tabletop, although he made no move to touch either. He moved like a puppet in response to the good news and bad news the telescreen delivered to him. His eyes became moist as an old song interrupted the newsflash. As it faded, so too did any trace of intelligence in Smith's eyes.

It had been the saddest, most frightening of the worlds I had had to visit and I felt no regrets when I stepped into a side street a kilometre from Miniluv and disappeared. In a thousand years it would be the same: there, as in so few other worlds, they had perfected death-in-life and purified the language of the tribe.

·WINSTON RUMFOORD·

There was only one place to meet Rumfoord.

Stepping from the flux of the void I felt the warm softness of sand, yielding beneath my weight; smelt the sweet scent of Titanic daisies clustered by the shoreline of the Winston Sea. Dominating the landscape before me was a large building, identical in appearance to the Taj Mahal. Behind it in the bright sky, Saturn was a huge ball of coloured gases, the broad swathe of its rings cutting through its bulk.

I began to walk towards 'Dun Roamin', the massive marble palace and, by its crystal pool, found Winston Niles Rumfoord, founder of the Church of God the Utterly Indifferent and author of THE POCKET HISTORY OF MARS.

Rumfoord was sprawled in his lavender contour chair by the side of the pool. Beside him his constant companion, the faithful mastiff Kazak, lay with his nose protruding over the water, whimpering gently in some realm of dog-dream. Rumfoord was, of course, expecting me. He was not 'punctual', which is to say he did not live his life sequentially, but was conscious at all times of everything that had and would happen to him. Earlier in his life, Rumfoord had driven his personal rocketship into a chrono-synclastic infundibulum on the way from Earth to Mars. The effect of this 'accident' was to spread Winston Niles Rumfoord and his dog Kazak across time and space in a spiral between Sol and Betelgeuse.

"I suppose the Muir discipline is something like a chrono-synclastic infundibulum. One you can more readily control. But the effect seems the same. You become non-punctual."

I knew that he could read minds and he, reading my mind, knew that I knew. He did not introduce himself and he knew both who I was and what it was that I wanted. I gazed down into the depths of the pool and, momentarily, studied the three statues of beautiful women, formed in the diamond-hard Titanic peat, which rested, like beckoning sirens, on the pool's floor. Elsewhere, on small islands of matter scattered frugally throughout the vast tracts of empty space between Sol and Betelgeuse, Rumfoord would be briefly materializing – taking on a momentarily solid form – before the spiralling chrono-synclastic infundibulum carried his fragmented self on elsewhere. When I met him there was slight sunspot activity and, while I watched,

parts of him seemed to swirl, become translucent, and then solidify again. He admitted to a faint nausea.

"Ah, but you should see me when I finally leave this Solar System! That is a regular firework show! The St Elmo's fire will dance brightly about me then, and I shall just . . . slowly . . . dis – appear . . ."

I found myself another sun chair and drew it up close to his. Salo, the Tralfamadorian alien, was elsewhere – making a group of statues about two miles off across the Sea.

"Something he saw in his viewer. Unk and Bee and Chrono. Oh, I would have been in it too, but I was hiding up a tree at the time."

I saw the group of statues later and realised that Salo had commemorated the moment when Unk had been told that he was really Malachi Constant, formerly the richest man on Earth, and the most despised. There was a long story behind that climactic moment; one that the machine-like Salo could barely comprehend. To understand it one would have to read Rumfoord's account of the pathetic invasion of Earth by a suicidal Martian army, and the subsequent scathing commentary by Dr Maurice Rosenau concerning Rumfoord's new Religion. They had all been sorely used, it seemed. Salo's statues were imbued with a symbolic and deeply human meaning incomprehensible to the Tralfamadorian. One would need to be human and tragically flawed to understand the mounted skeleton of the mastiff, the good-luck piece in Chrono's young hands, and the yellow-green suit with the orange question-marks that Unk/Malachi wore.

It was hard to know if Rumfoord were watching me behind his dark-tinted glasses. His right hand rested in Kazak's coat, the end of the choke chain visible about his wrist. In his other hand a cigarette was held firm in a long ivory holder, as yet unlit. There was an unnatural passivity about him, as if he had been (as it seemed, perhaps, he was) blighted by a most severe fatalism. It must have been like reading from a script for him.

"I can blank it all out for most of the time. My problem is not remembering, but forgetting. It's all there, all of the time, jumbled and senseless – like white noise – unless I forget. For me, the mind's time-bound, punctual protection has ceased to be effective. I'm Time's dupe!"

The glottal tenor of Rumfoord's voice was a soft yodel as he spoke. He seemed, for a moment, to gaze at his slightly calloused palm, as if to recollect something amongst the jumble of his life. A golden thread danced briefly between his fingers and then was gone. It was difficult to bear in mind that, at that same moment, Rumfoord was appearing in the deep caves of Mercury or, for an hour, in the tiny chimney room of the big house in Newport, Rhode Island.

"The big question always is – are you being used, or are you the one doing the using? Who, for instance, was using Noel Constant when he built up his financial empire? Who is using me? Who you? And if Tralfamadore uses the whole human race and its history to deliver a single spaceship part, who then is using *them* for some meagre, unsuspecting purpose?"

If I had not known Rumfoord's curious history beforehand I might have suspected that he was a callous madman. His disappearance down the rabbit-hole of Space and Time – deliberate or otherwise – appeared to have been a quite tragic affair at first examination.

"But does tragedy itself exist? If everything is fixed and determined beforehand, as my own case would seem to bear out, doesn't everything then come under the heading of 'necessity'? Perhaps it is unprofitable even to pursue such matters: we do not seem able to *change* things, and the efforts we expend in *trying* to change things can only provoke us to fury when we discover that all our efforts have been to no avail. I sometimes feel that the whole essence of life lies somewhere between the infructuous and the infuriating."

With a sudden movement, Rumfoord got up out of his chair and, his dog Kazak stirring from its half sleep and growling a warning at me, I followed the two of them down to the water's edge where a small rowing boat was awaiting us. On the mainland we disembarked and made our way to Salo's crippled spacecraft.

Inside the saucer, Rumfoord sat himself in the lounger before the great screen and activated a few of the controls. Instantly we were watching an earlier moment in the life of Winston Niles Rumfoord, and then, as now, he was to be seen in his habitual posture of decadent relaxation, the result of two centuries of breeding.

What we were witnessing was the fateful and suicidal attack on Earth by the inefficient Martian army. The super-modern flying saucers (modelled on Salo's ship) concealed an army that was armed with the most archaic of modern weaponry. Most of the invasion fleet had been blown out of the air before they ever got near Earth.

"God, if he was the least bit interested, could have prevented that. As he doesn't give a damn, however, we have to take good care of ourselves and create our own racial conscience."

He adjusted the touch-plate controls that rested by his left hand and in a few moments we were looking into Skip's Museum, the small chimney room on the Rumfoord Estate. In the screen we watched a young, tousle-haired boy paint letters on a driftwood plank in a bright blue. Behind him, on a rickety table, was a collection of variously-shaped shells and the bones of wild animals: things the young boy had undoubtedly found on the beaches of Narragansett Bay and in the woods about

Plate 1. *With Saturn looming large in Titan's sky, down by the shore of the Winston Sea, Winston Niles Rumfoord makes his final departure from the solar system, to spiral off elsewhere in the Universe, following his dog, Kazak. A pale green cocoon of light encloses the whole scene as the St Elmo's fire plays over Rumfoord's immaculately-dressed figure*

Plate 2. *Rumfoord, surrounded by the second wave of the Martian invasion fleet of Earth, watches the impending obliteration of the first wave by nuclear devices. The flying saucer was modelled on the craft belonging to the Tralfamadorian, Salo, itself based on a design 801,885,000 years old. Rumfoord's perverse orchestration of events nonetheless brought Peace on Earth for the first time ever.*

Plate 3. *Bee (Winston's former wife, Beatrice) and her son, Chrono, walk away from Malachi Constant, who, at one time, was the richest man on Earth. But as Unk, an unaware Martian soldier, he had suffered the utmost humiliation at Rumfoord's hands. Here, in his enigmatic costume, he walks towards the Titan-bound spacecraft. Bee and Chrono were to go with him into exile.*

Newport. The boy was Skip, the youthful Winston Niles Rumfoord.

"Salo always pretends that my arrival here on Titan was an accident. Yet here, in the memory store of this screen, he has more than fifteen hundred sequences from my childhood."

Rumfoord laughed humourlessly and drew at his cigarette. Then he looked directly at me.

"Isn't *that* a gross irony? To discover that the ultimate in technological advancement is to create a self-deluding machine!"

I knew Rumfoord's hostility towards Salo's mechanical origins. He showed me perhaps two dozen clips of himself as a child, and I noticed in the boy that same, unmistakable charismatic quality of natural charm that was so immediately evident in the grown man.

One of the final sequences he focused upon was of himself in his early twenties, looking debonair in a light brown tweed jacket and matching pants. Beside him as he walked along the garden path towards the fountain, was a young girl dressed in a full length, brilliant white dress. The girl's features were harshly drawn, like those of an Indian squaw. When she spoke (for she never seemed to smile) she revealed not only the unusual length of her teeth, but also a remarkable distance between herself and the imperfection of the real world. It was Beatrica, Winston's partner in his unconsummated marriage. Later, as Bee, she would become Malachi/Unk's mate.

"Later, Now, Earlier . . . what do these terms *mean*? Do we define the order by simple cause and effect, or are we just seeing it all wrong? Are the effects *really* the causes and the causes the effects?"

In everything he did, Rumfoord seemed to display a natural sense of style and gallantry. They were pervasive to his very existence. We were walking back to the rowing boat, Kazak snuffling the ground, faint sparks flickering in his coat as the sun-spots became active once again. I had asked him what he felt was an unusual question: had he enjoyed his life? Was it so bad to be used by some greater agency (for such was his view)?

"Enjoyment seems a rather irrelevant concept now. I suppose I must have enjoyed myself when I was still punctual. Ignorance has its blessings, you know. I remember my childhood with fondness. My parents were remote, god-like figures. I suppose I ought to have suffered from their neglect, but there were always the servants to play German batball with and the pleasure of Skip's Museum to keep me fully occupied. Don't believe anyone when they say money and breeding can't buy happiness. There's a very good reason why they're saying it!"

We both knew that it was time for me to get off of the particular roller-coaster I was momentarily riding with Rumfoord. We said our goodbyes back beside the crystal pool, the sirens below us, beneath the water.

"Part of me says goodbye to part of you. Though why, I can't fathom. You'll always be here and I'll always be here too. Rather like characters in a book. You come back years later and they're still there: same scene, same words, same actions."

It was an interesting thought to take with me. I recalled the ancient belief in fiction I had so lightly dismissed at the start of my travels. Perhaps there was something, after all, to be said for it. I smiled, and, like the Cheshire Cat, vanished.

· HOWARD LESTER ·

Howard Lester's account of his explorations of the psychic realm was complete only up to the middle of the 1970's, and I was determined to discover what had happened since the end of that document. When I knocked at the large oak door of Langton Place, the old vicarage at Great Glen in Leicestershire, I was met by Sir Henry Littleway, Lester's constant companion in his investigations.

"I've been expecting you. I've sensed something all day. Howard isn't here. He's at the Carter Institute. But he'll meet you there."

I had anticipated such a welcome. Littleway's development of his mental powers was second only to that of his friend. I thanked him and returned to the hired car. The youthful-looking Littleway gave no further attention to me. He had returned inside just as soon as he had delivered his message. It was November 1995 and I had learned already that Littleway and Lester had formed a society, the Carter Institute, named after their generous benefactor, Sir Robert Carter, himself the author of "Reflexions", a book of psychic insights, and an expert on Japanese mysticism. Travelling up the new fast-traffic Intercity motorway to Newcastle, I recollected what I already knew of Lester's past and of his plans for the future.

Howard Lester had been born in 1942, of humble parentage, but his precocious thirst for knowledge had, at thirteen, introduced him to the patronage of Sir Alastair Lyell, who, until his death in 1967, was Howard's substitute father and companion in studies. Howard had been the amanuensis of Lyell, helping him in the laboratory in his various studies. Through Lyell's example, Howard had developed an eclectic mind, embracing every aspect of knowledge that was open to him. Lester's life path, after Lyell's death, had been an erratic one. For several years afterwards, he had struggled to maintain some sense of order in his studies, occasionally succumbing to his despair and drinking heavily. From an early age, however, he had had a fascination with death and immortality, and his investigations in this sphere had brought him gradually to the conclusion that Man could overcome death by maintaining his intellectual vitality and exercising his *will*.

Lyell's will had provided Howard with a secure financial situation, and he was able to dedicate his life thereafter, as he had before, to whatever line of studies he wished to follow. He in fact chose to investigate longevity, and where at first his enquiries were of a scientific nature, looking into the functions of the *autolytic enzymes,* they eventually turned to the writings of the mystics and through them to 'value experiences' and the work of Sir Henry Littleway and his associates.

Lester's association with Littleway was an extraordinary one. Together they investigated the properties of the mind and discovered a means of amplifying its latent psychic powers. At first this was achieved mechanically, with fragments of Neumann's alloy, but later it was found by Howard that it could be done merely by mental exercise. As they experimented with the new clarity of mental vision this technique allowed them, they realised that it was a means not only of increasing their intellectual power, but also of enabling them to *see* the Past and to create perfect images of memorised items. Through their developing powers they had become like Siamese twins, and had formed a psychic link between them. It was this link (and his *awareness*) that had allowed Littleway to greet me without introduction. He *knew* all that was in my conscious mind (*though I shielded knowledge of my curious origins from him carefully*).

Later, as I parked my gascar beneath the huge Institute building in Princess Square, I sensed Howard's greeting in my mind and returned it. Very soon I was sitting beside him in the penthouse bar, sipping a brandy (alone, for he had long since ceased taking artificial stimulants) as he talked about his successes in the twenty years since he had written his autobiography.

"As a boy I was an isolated and rather arrogant young fellow," he began. *In his pale blue one-piece suit he looked little more than twenty-five, though I knew that he was fifty-three.* "My father and brothers hated me. Perhaps rightly so. But that could not be helped. I sensed even then that Man must either progress upward or stagnate. And stagnation is death."

The apparent lack of emotion he had suffered as a child was not in evidence in the mature man. Beside him as we talked was his wife, Barbara. The smiles they shared were communications of deep mutual understanding. But it was not confined to them alone. In the comparative quiet of the building (for the urban Britain of 1995 was extremely noisy) several thousands of his acolytes shared a growing web of awareness. At one point in our conversation Howard apologised briefly and then went into a fifteen minute trance. When he had 'returned' he explained (even though I recognised it quite well) that several times a day they would all link minds to concentrate upon a single image – one that grew in complexity as each new member of the Institute added their own chosen emblem to the total design. He was about to launch into an explanation of the Old Ones – the gods of ancient Earth who had been sleeping now for six million years and who, he was certain, were soon to waken – when he caught a glimpse of the foreknowledge of it in my mind. With that glimpse he became interested in me and asked if I had taken a similar path to him in developing my mental powers. I described circumstances that were, in effect, merely adaptations of his own past and by that means made him talk about the days in

Plate 1. *After the death of the labourer, Dick O'Sullivan, Howard Lester had gone down to his weekend cottage at Rochford to revivify his spirits. Whilst there, on one of his late night walks by the water's edge, he realised the web-like interconnection of all things. The significance of the value experiences he had been investigating was suddenly revealed to him and, from the depths of despair, he was raised to new heights of awareness. It was a state of vivid illumination and of acute focus. Standing there he realised that the direction of man's evolution was from the animal to the god. From then on he concentrated his investigations on the brain itself.*

which he had spent hours exploring the extent of his unfolding mental powers.

His fondest memory, and one that he recalls as the most invigorating in his book, was of the time he spent in the cottage near Rochford in Essex. He had rested there for the whole of a month after the death of the farm labourer, Dick O'Sullivan, whom he and Littleway had been experimenting upon. From an initial feeling of acute depression he had rebuilt his morale and realised that he was on the verge of a breakthrough. As the sun set over the water, he had his first intuition about the web-like nature of man's consciousness.

"I only have to visualise that scene and I am back there, on the beach at sunset, looking at my past self as I stand poised before taking that giant leap forward; that unleashing of the powers of the mind."

I could only postpone his questions, however, for his keen mind penetrated my superficial barriers. I explained that I was Gregory Lyell, a nephew of the Aubrey Lyell he had once spent several weeks with in Alexandria, prior to his breakthrough.

"Then you too must have read Canon Lyell's book on mysticism," he said to me. "How close he was and yet how far away from the truth. Not only can we train men to exercise their full psychic potential, but we can breed *new* men who are born with their full powers, unfettered."

Howard's son, Tom, was introduced to me later in the day. He had been named after Howard's younger brother who had died the year he was born. Howard's mother and father were also long dead, and only his elder brother, Arnold remained of his direct kin.

"To *make* oneself a new man, one has also, unfortunately, to *make* oneself a new family," he explained. But there seemed little regret in his tone. He had always sensed an alienation from the 'sleepers', as he called all of those not of the Institute. I asked him how the Institute had fared and why he had found it necessary to have substantial financial support. "Rob" (*as he called Sir Robert Carter*) "bought us time and privacy. Without his influence we would have been the target of every politician short-sighted enough to see us as a power-hungry clique of elitists. We must build the new man before the Old Ones waken. Only the pettiness of the 'sleepers' can prevent that." But his intention was not, as it might seem, to *exclude* the 'sleepers' from his web. "Eventually all of mankind will awaken to this new evolutionary stage. It may take generations. Those who cannot adapt will eventually die . . . but of natural causes. It will be a painless process."

There was one other thing, however, that I wished to ask him, another aspect of his power that I sought more knowledge of. Had he, like K'tholo, the powerful ancient priest of the Old Ones, let his mind wander out into the Cosmos to explore the

Plate 2. *When on his occasional visits to Aubrey Lyell, whose large house on the outskirts of Alexandria contained copies of the famous Canon Lyell's collection of mystical writings, he would go out into the nearby desert late at night and focus upon the surrounding universe, letting his mind wander far outward. Often his wife Barbara and his best friend, Sir Henry Littleway, would join with him and extend a web of their consciousness to embrace all of the nearer stars, touching the emergent awarenesses of other, newer beings. As is evident in the picture, Lester, though in his late fifties, had never aged after his mid-twenties. He claimed that the development of Man's psychic potential was the key to Immortality.*

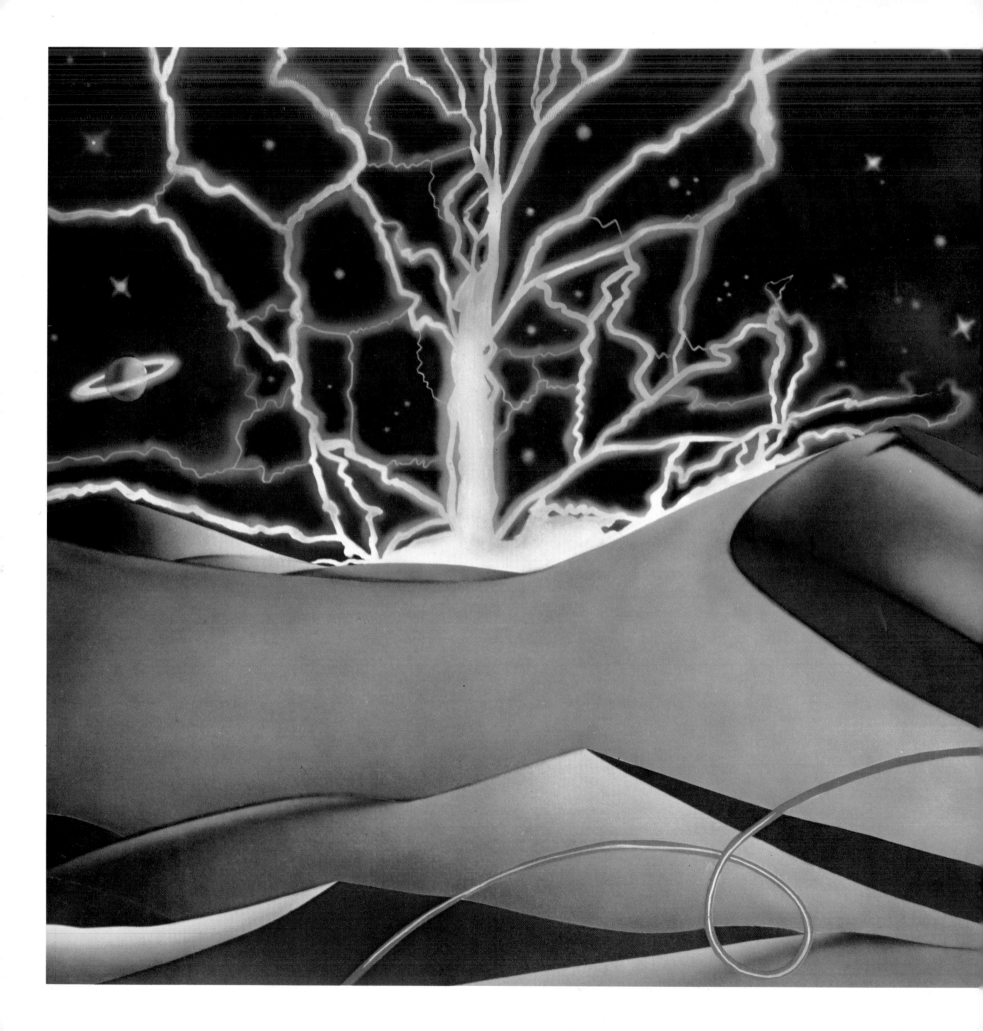

planets? He grinned at me and laughed heartily, glimpsing perhaps the vaguest hint of my own much-travelled mind.

"You seem to ask me much of what you already know. I could almost believe that you were one of the *new men* of the Future, come back in Time to question me. You are impossible to read – as difficult as the Mayan figurine from the well of Chichen Itza."

He probed me no further on this point, and instead complied with my wishes, telling me of his frequent visits to Alexandria (*and from this alone I realised that my pose as Gregory Lyell had not, for a moment, fooled him*). He would stand alone in the cold desert nights of Southern Egypt and let his mind reach upward and outward into the solar system and beyond. Alone he could not venture very far, but on occasions he would summon the assistance of Barbara and Littleway, and together they would penetrate the vacuum between the stars, linked by a strong psychic thread from mind to mind as they stretched the web of their awareness to encompass several light-years of space.

As I made my farewells, the music, which had been a constant gentle presence in the background throughout our talk, momentarily increased in volume. "Ah, the Fantasia on a theme by Thomas Tallis" Lester informed me. "Ralph Vaughan Williams. Pure nostalgia for me. Almost a reminiscence of childhood now." But there was no wistfulness and I sensed that Howard Lester was not greatly moved by nostalgia or by any of the more 'common' forms of emotion. I left him with no clue to Muir's 'solution'. In Howard Lester's universe the Old Ones *would* eventually awaken, to find the *new man* only partly prepared for their coming.

I drove the gascar into a secluded side street, settled back in the driving seat and began the series of mental disciplines which would carry me to my final destination.

·EPILOGUE·

All time and all space swirled about me, formless, colourless, and then, with an immediacy which only strict discipline can accustom one to, I was standing once again on G82, the *Daniel Martin* building less than a dozen paces from me. It was early morning and the plaza was empty. Primitive bird forms sang their peculiar, repetitive songs beyond the safety barrier and the dark, primordial forest that surrounded the tiny settlement seemed to bristle with emergent life. I mounted the stairs and made my way up to the de-briefing room. There, throughout the rest of the day, I dictated my reports and edited them to the concise form I knew Muir required of us. Other students sat near to me, freshly returned from other ventures in other worlds and other times. They would sit in profound meditation, ordering the masses of thoughts and impressions they had returned with, to give solid form to chaos just as I tried to give definite shape to the complex personalities I had met on my travels.

Had my long apprenticeship fully prepared me for the experience of travelling amongst the possibility worlds? It was a question I had been set by Muir at the very outset of my training and only now, my first assignment complete, could I answer. My training had prepared me to encounter radically different worlds and their accompanying modes of thought, but it had not provided me with the essential spark of imagination needed to empathise with the people I had met. I had needed to provide that spark myself. I was reminded of Muir's comments on the role of fiction back on Earth-Prime. I recalled that there had been people who dismissed fiction (just as they had dismissed dreams) as worthless and unproductive. I realised now that fiction (just as dreams before it) was an evolutionary step: the first stage in freeing the mind from its time-bonding.

When I had finished editing my reports I punched the Final button and received the neat-print hardcopy from the desk unit before me. Making my way back down the stairs to Muir's office I was conscious of a feeling of profound satisfaction. It was only my first of a great many such assignments, yet I knew that it would be the one I would always recall with greatest fondness and clarity. Muir's secretary waved me through – he was expecting me. I went on in and sat across from him.

"I only have to look at your face to see how much you've enjoyed yourself. Perhaps you understand now why I've always emphasised the need for sympathy, tolerance and understanding."

He was grinning as widely as I, and in his mild Glaswegian accent he went on to tell *me* what I had *really* discovered on my first trip amongst the possibility worlds.

"Lawrence once said 'Thought is not a trick, or an exercise, or a set of dodges. Thought is a man in his wholeness wholly attending.' The same is true for imagination which, as you and I know from experience now, is the most important aspect of thought. Man must dream to live and, eventually, he will live to dream . . . in a manner of speaking."

As I sat there I had the sudden, vivid image of the old pre-dreaming man, still seated on his Rome-bound express, confined by the track of time.

"As you doubtlessly guessed, fiction is the triggering device; the means by which man will make his upward evolutionary step. Our task is merely to suggest. Thus your report will become a book – a piece of their 'fiction' for some to scoff at and others to marvel. And so, by such means, we shall slowly remove the barriers that prevent Man from fully realising his dreaming potential."

Thirty thousand years in the past the first of a new breed of Man was stepping onto a train at Victoria Station. I smiled at the thought.

· A C K N O W L E D G E M E N T S ·

This book would not have been possible without the imaginative efforts of the authors listed below. To them must go my gratitude and respect for their original creations. If you have read the books from which these characters are drawn I hope you will enjoy the additional information given here. If you have not read the books, I hope you will want to do so at the earliest opportunity.

The sources for 'The Immortals' are as follows:

SUSAN CALVIN	*I, Robot*
	The Rest Of The Robots
	by Isaac Asimov
THE ILLUSTRATED MAN	*The Illustrated Man*
	by Ray Bradbury
SLIPPERY JIM DIGRIZ	*The Stainless Steel Rat*
	The Stainless Steel Rat's Revenge
	The Stainless Steel Rat Saves The World
	The Stainless Steel Rat Wants You
	by Harry Harrison
LEWIS ORNE	*The Godmakers*
	by Frank Herbert
OSCAR GORDON	*Glory Road*
	by Robert Heinlein
ESAU CAIRN	*Almuric*
	by Robert E. Howard
BEOWULF SHAEFFER	*Neutron Star*
	Tales Of Known Space
	by Larry Niven
WINSTON SMITH	*Nineteen Eighty-Four*
	by George Orwell
WINSTON RUMFOORD	*The Sirens Of Titan*
	by Kurt Vonnegut
HOWARD LESTER	*The Philosopher's Stone*
	by Colin Wilson